# THE RED RIBBON GIRLS

ADAM J. WRIGHT

D1739217

**ALSO BY ADAM J. WRIGHT**

DARK PEAK

# THE
# RED
# RIBBON
# GIRLS

# CHAPTER 1

The flat isn't perfect but that somehow makes me love it even more. *Perfect would be boring*, I tell myself as I step through the open door. The imperfections tell the stories of past tenants. Like the little dent in the wall, just inside the front door. It was probably made when the last people moved out; maybe they dinged the wall with the corner of their sofa as they struggled to get it out into the hallway, leaving a permanent mark of their stay here.

Had they loved this flat as much as I'm sure I will love it? Or had they left under a cloud and crept away into the rainy night?

The landlord, who lives in the basement and who doesn't seem old enough to be a landlord, hadn't been forthcoming about why the previous tenants left. "It doesn't matter why they're gone," he said when Greg and I came to view the flat for the first time. "The point is, the flat is available. Do you want it or not?" He knew he had the upper hand. If we didn't want the flat, there were plenty of people who would. It wasn't every day you found a well-appointed flat with off-road parking in a huge Victorian building situated near the seaside town of Whitby. Northmoor House may have been split up into flats now but it's still a magnificent building and each of its three floors is spacious, with more than enough room for a couple like me and Greg or even a small family.

The sea view alone—not to mention the picturesque view of the North Yorkshire Moors through the rear windows—would make anyone snap up this place in a heartbeat.

Which is what we did, and now this view belongs to us.

I walk over to the big Victorian sash window and gaze out at the cliffs and the hazy, wintery horizon. There are dark clouds out there, in the distance, moving inland. They'll reach us soon, along with a barrage of snow, probably. I won't let it spoil my day. If it snows, it snows. By the time it gets here, all our furniture should be safe inside anyway, and then I can sit here with a steaming mug of hot chocolate and watch the flakes melting on the window, blurring the outside world.

There's a window box and even though there aren't any flowers in it at the moment, I imagine how colourful it will look when I've planted it with purple hyacinths and red tulips.

"You daydreaming again?"

I turn to see Greg standing at the door, hands on his hips, one eyebrow cocked in amusement.

"Maybe," I say, smiling. "I'm just thinking about all the times I'll get to stare out at this incredible view."

"Well just as long as you don't spend *all* your time staring at the view. Gazing at the sea won't pay the rent." He joins me at the window and lets out a low whistle. "That's some storm heading this way. They'd better get our stuff inside pretty soon."

"I'm sure they will," I say, unable to believe that anything could go wrong today. It's a day filled with promises and anticipation and marks the first day of our new life. Everything will go as planned and the furniture will remain dry.

"Hmm, I'm not so sure," Greg says, turning away from the window and heading for the door.

"The removal men are complaining about the stairs and the fact that most of our stuff won't fit in the lift." He peers out into the hallway. "Maybe I should go down there and tell them to get their fingers out."

"I'm sure they know what they're doing."

He turns back to me and narrows his eyes. "What are you on today?"

"Nothing, what do you mean?"

"Moving house is one of the most stressful things you can do in life but you're wandering around like you don't have a care in the world."

"I'm just happy, that's all. Don't you think living here is going to be amazing?"

He looks around the room and shrugs. "It would be more amazing if there wasn't mould on the bathroom tiles."

"I know the flat isn't perfect but doesn't that make it somehow more lovable?"

"No, it makes it more damp."

The sound of a *thud* comes from down the hallway, followed by a muttered curse.

"Sounds like the sofa has arrived," Greg says. He steps aside, allowing the two removal men to manoeuvre the sofa into the flat. They set it down in the middle of the room and then, after throwing each other a look that says they regret ever taking this job, disappear back through the doorway.

"Maybe I should make them a cup of tea," I suggest. "It can't be easy for them, having to carry everything up two flights of stairs."

"It's only the big stuff," Greg says. "The rest of it should fit into the lift. Besides, you can't make a cup of tea, the kettle is packed away in one of the boxes."

"No, it isn't" I tell him, shaking my head. "It's in my car, along with the tea bags and a pint of milk. I unpacked it because I thought we might like a cuppa when we arrive."

Greg grins. "That's just like you, prepared for anything. Okay, let's put our feet up and have a brew. At least we have somewhere to sit now." He drops down onto the sofa and lets out a long sigh.

"Anyone would think *you'd* carried the sofa up here," I tell him, patting him playfully on the head as I pass him and go out of the door.

Once I'm in the hallway, I wonder if I should go down the stairs or take the lift. I'm not sure I trust the rickety-looking contraption that sits at the end of the hallway behind a wrought iron gate but I suppose it must be in good working order. There are laws and building regulations to make sure tenants aren't put in danger, after all.

Still, I decide to take the stairs and veer past the lift to the top of the staircase. But as I take the first couple of steps down, I realise the removal men are coming up with an armchair. There's no way I'm going to be able to squeeze past them.

I hesitate, wondering if I should wait for them to bring the chair up but then I hear a bang and one of the men says, "Bloody hell, Tony, be careful! You nearly bloody killed me! We need to take it nice and slow, okay?"

*The lift it is, then.*

I turn to the wrought iron gate and slide it aside. The metal clangs loudly, uninvitingly, as if warning me away. I step inside and realise why the removal men were complaining; there's barely enough room for two people in here, never mind large pieces of furniture.

The control panel, a stainless steel plate bolted to the wall, bears three metal buttons: *2,1,G*. I press G for the ground floor and wait. Nothing happens. I press the button again. The lift remains unmoved by the action.

"Bloody thing," I curse under my breath. As I'm about to step out, I remember that I haven't closed the gate. There's probably a safety catch or something that won't allow the lift to work while the gate is open. I slide it shut, feeling claustrophobic as it locks into place with an ominous-sounding *click*.

Praying the lift won't take long to reach the ground floor, I try pressing the button again.

I hear a low mechanical grinding sound from somewhere in the building and then a high-pitched squeal as the cables begin to move under protest. The lift lurches beneath my feet and begins its descent. Slowly.

It takes almost 30 seconds to rumble down from the second floor to the first. As the first floor hallway comes into view, I wonder who lives here, beneath us. Maybe it's someone we'll make friends with. Our first friends in Whitby.

The lift continues its slow descent and the first floor disappears, to be replaced, half a minute later, with the ground floor hallway and the building's front door. My sigh of relief catches in my throat as I notice that another door—the one that leads to the basement flat—is also open. Rob North, the landlord, is leaning against the doorjamb, arms folded, his eyes staring directly at me from behind his glasses.

We've learned from the lease that the building is actually owned by a Fred and Wanda North, who live in Spain. We've surmised that Fred and Wanda retired to the Continent and left their son Rob in charge, probably allowing him to live in the basement flat as part of the deal. I try not to make quick judgements regarding people but Rob creeped me out from the moment I met him. He seems to be surrounded by a cloud of body odour and his skin is so pasty, it's almost white. He looks as if he never gets out of his basement during daylight hours. His greasy long hair, sticking out from beneath a baseball cap, and the crumb-covered Star Wars T-shirt draped over his weighty frame add to the impression that he's a gamer who spends most of his time sitting in front of a computer screen.

*Did he hear the lift and come up here to meet me?* I suddenly wished I'd taken the stairs. I'll definitely be taking them in future because I don't want this guy being here every time I leave the flat. I tell myself I might be overreacting but there's something about the landlord's posture that suggests he's waiting here for me.

The lift comes to a dead stop and I slide the noisy gate aside.

"Hey, Katy," Rob says, offering me a short wave.

"It's Kate," I tell him firmly. I haven't been called Katy since I was ten-years-old, when my younger brother Max was still alive. Since Max's death, no one else has ever called me Katy; I haven't allowed them to.

"Oh right," Rob says, nodding. "Kate." He licks his lips as if tasting my name.

*Maybe I'm overreacting. Maybe he's just trying to be friendly and I'm misreading it. God knows I've misread situations before...*

*Just get to the car and get the kettle.*

I walk past Rob, trying to ignore the creeping sensation that crawls over my back as I pass him. Once the door is open and a blast of bitter, fresh air hits my face, I feel more confident and risk a look back into the building. Rob is gone, his door closed.

Now, I feel a bit silly. I just breezed past the poor guy like I was too good to talk to him or something.

Outside, a strong, cold wind blows across the gravelled parking area, heralding the storm which I can now see is closer than before. I walk around the removal van and stride over to my Mini, retrieving a small cardboard box containing the kettle, tea bags, six mugs, and a pint of milk from the boot.

As I close the boot, I notice something on the moors, a flash of bright colour in the distance. Squinting, I see dozens of yellow hi-vis jackets and a couple of white Land Rovers. The police are out there, moving slowly across the land like a swarm of neon wasps in search of sugar. But the police aren't looking for anything sweet, I realise with a sudden shock. They must be searching for Amy Donovan, a young woman who went missing from this area two days ago.

I've heard about Amy's disappearance on the TV News but haven't taken much notice of the latest developments in the search for her because I've been so busy packing and getting ready for the move. Seeing the police here, though, so close to my new home, makes it all seem suddenly real.

I watch the police for a few moments, wondering what the parents of Amy Donovan must be feeling. The anguish must be crushing them. At this point, the police are probably expecting to find a body, their hope of finding Amy alive slipping away with each passing hour.

I turn away from the scene and quickly make my

way back into the building, the box tucked under my arm. I half expect to see Rob at his door waiting for me but he isn't there. I breathe a sigh of relief.

But as I walk toward the stairs, I hear a door open behind me. Certain that he's come out to talk to me, I put my head down and increase my pace slightly.

"Have you seen my cat?"

The voice is that of a woman. I stop in my tracks and turn around to see that the open door isn't Rob's at all but a door on the opposite side of the hallway. Probably the ground floor flat.

An old woman has stepped out. She's smartly dressed in a blue floral blouse beneath a white cardigan and a long dark blue skirt. Her hair is white and tightly-curled, her face worn and wrinkled, but there's a spark in her dark eyes that belies her age. She holds an open tin of tuna in one hand and a fork in the other.

"Have you seen him?" she asks. "He's ginger. I don't like to think of him outside in this weather. There's a storm coming, you know."

"Yes, I know," I tell her. "It's quite blustery out there."

She nods. "That's why he has to come home.

He can't be out there in the snow. What if he gets a cold?"

I'm sure the cat will find shelter long before the storm gets here but I can't bear to think of the old lady sitting in her flat fretting about him.

"I'll have a look for him," I suggest, placing my box on the floor next to her open door. Her flat is cosy-looking, filled with furniture and framed photographs. I can smell a cake baking in the kitchen, the sweet aroma of sponge and coconut making my stomach rumble.

She smiles at me. "Thank you, dear, that's very kind of you. I'm not so good on my feet these days."

"Well you go and sit down and I'll look for your cat. What's his name?"

"Winston." She hands me the tuna and the fork solemnly, as if bestowing a great responsibility onto me. "If you tap on the tin he might come to you. If not, you'll have to search for him, I'm afraid. He likes to hide."

"I'm sure I'll find him," I tell her, although I don't feel as confident as my words might suggest. I step out into the wind, tapping on the tin and calling the cat's name. Winston doesn't appear. He probably has more sense than to be out in this weather and is snuggled up somewhere safe and warm.

The door swings open and the two removal men come outside, sweating and panting after wrestling the armchair up the stairs. One of them sees me and grins. "Nearly there, love." He and his colleague climb into the back of the van.

I try to guess where a cat might hide around here but there aren't any obvious spots. The parking area is just a flat gravelled area and beyond that, the moors stretch away into the distance. I tap the tin again and call out, "Winston. Come on, Winston."

This time there is a response but instead of seeing Winston come running out from under one of the cars, I hear one of the removal men shout, "Bloody hell there's a cat in here!"

I hear a flurry of movement in the van and then a fat ginger tomcat jumps out, licking his lips either in indignation of being ejected from the van —where he was no doubt snuggled in among our furniture—or from anticipation as he smells the tuna in the tin. He runs over to me, purring, and rubs his head and body against my jeans, walking around my legs in a tight circle and looking up at me with big green eyes.

"Come on," I say, "let's get you inside." I open the door and he runs in ahead of me.

"Winston!" the old lady says, leaning over to scratch between the cat's ears. She looks up at me with an appreciative smile. "Thank you, dear. Would you like some cake?"

"I'd love some," I say, "but I really must get back upstairs. My name's Kate, by the way. Kate Lumley. We're moving in upstairs." I hold out my hand.

She shakes it, her fingers as cold as icicles. "I'm Ivy. Pop down anytime you want a cup of tea and a chat."

"I will," I tell her, handing her the tin of tuna and the fork.

She goes into her flat, talking to the cat in a soft voice, and closes the door. I pick my box up off the floor and make my way to the stairs, glad that I've already made a friend. Two friends if you count Winston.

As I pass Rob North's door, I see a spy hole at eye level. None of the other doors in the building seem to have one of those, only his.

And I can't shake the feeling that he's standing behind the door right now, staring through it.

Watching me.

# CHAPTER 2

The storm hits us an hour later. The wind rattles the windows and throws hail and snow at the glass. The hailstones bounce off the panes like a thousand tiny marbles. I'm sitting in the armchair, by the same window I'd looked out of earlier. I don't have the mug of hot chocolate I'd promised myself because I'm not sure which box contains the contents of our kitchen cupboard. So the mug in my hand contains tea made with slightly sour milk.

All of our furniture is safely in the flat, the removal men long gone. Greg is standing at the rear window, looking out over the moors. He's been standing there for at least ten minutes, seemingly transfixed by something.

"What are you looking at?" I ask him.

"The police."

"Are they still out there? In this?"

He nods and takes a sip of his tea. "They're persistent."

"Well that's good." If it was my loved one that was lost, that's what I'd want them to be: persistent. I join Greg at the window and watch the bright yellow hi-vis jackets move across the windswept moors. The grass and the heather is hidden beneath a sparkling white blanket of snow. "Do you think they'll find her?"

He frowns. "Find who?"

"That woman. Amy Donovan. That must be what they're doing, right? Looking for Amy?"

He shrugs. "I don't know. Who's Amy Donovan?"

"The woman that went missing. We saw it on the News, remember?" But then *I* remember that Greg was at work when I saw the news report about Amy Donovan. The subject never came up in conversation until now. I'm surprised he hasn't heard anything about it on the TV or radio but we've been busy with the move and all of our attention has been on packing.

"Amy Donovan disappeared from one of the

villages near here a couple of days ago," I tell Greg. I can't remember the name of the village but I remember thinking it was only a few miles from here.

"Sounds a bit too close for comfort," Greg says.

"Yeah. She's been missing for two days and no one knows where she is."

"Well I'm sure the police will get to the bottom of it," he says, finishing his tea. He takes the mug into the kitchen and then I hear a loud groan. "Oh, you have got to be kidding me!"

"What is it?" I rush into the kitchen to find Greg looking up at the ceiling above the kitchen sink. A pool of water has formed there and drops are dripping into the sink. "Oh no."

He lets out a sigh. "I'll have to get the lad downstairs to come up and have a look at it."

"We don't have to do that now," I say, not wanting Rob North in the flat, at least not right now. "Look, it's dripping into the sink so it's not doing any damage to the kitchen."

I'm not sure if Greg is listening. He's staring up at the pool of water above his head and stroking his chin, deep in thought.

"The roof must be leaking into the attic," he says finally. He turns to the stacks of boxes by the fridge. "I think there's a bucket in here somewhere, isn't there?" He starts to rummage through the boxes.

"Yes, I think so. What are you going to do?"

He points at the ceiling. "I'm going to go up there and put a bucket down to catch the water. At least that'll stop it leaking into our flat."

This is just like Greg. As soon as he sees a problem, he leaps into action to fix it. I'm glad he's going to tackle the leak himself and not get the landlord up here.

He finds the bucket, and a small torch, and takes them into the living room, where his aluminium stepladder is leaning against the wall. Greg used the ladder when he was decorating our old flat in Manchester and insisted on bringing it with us when we decided to come to Whitby. At the time, I thought it would probably sit unused in our new home forever but he's found a use for it already.

"There must be an access hatch somewhere on this level," he says, "Probably out here somewhere." He opens the door and angles the stepladder out through the opening and into the hallway. I pick up the bucket and torch and follow him.

"Aha!" he says when he spies a hatch in the ceiling. It isn't a small hatch at all; it's a big oblong that runs almost half the length of the hallway. A small brass ring set into a brass plate seems to be the method by which it opens.

"I've seen these before," Greg says. "If I pull on that ring, the hatch pivots down like a ramp. There might even be steps. I won't need the ladder."

"You'll need it to reach the ring," I tell him, aware of a rumbling noise in the building. It sounds like someone is using the lift.

"Of course," he says. "You hold the ladder steady and we'll have this thing open in no time."

I don't share his enthusiasm; I don't want him climbing into an unknown loft. There could be anything up there. What if he cuts himself on something or, worse, falls through the ceiling?

He sets the ladder up underneath the brass ring, unfolding it until the metal supports lock into place and then pressing his hands down on the top step to assure himself it's secure. I take hold of it to keep it steady.

"Be careful, Greg."

"Careful is my middle name," he says, wiggling his eyebrows at me. "Hand me the torch."

I do so but as soon as Greg has his foot on the

bottom rung of the ladder, there's a shout from the end of the hallway. "Hey, you can't go up there!"

I turn in that direction to see Rob North in the lift, pulling back the iron gate. He has a face like thunder and his big hands are tightened into meaty fists. As soon as the gate is out of his way, he storms along the hallway towards us.

Greg steps down from the ladder. "I was just going up there to stop the water from leaking into our flat."

"You can't go up there," Rob repeats. "It's not allowed!"

"Okay, okay," Greg says, holding up his hands. I've seen him hold his own over much less—he once had a trolley rage incident with an old lady in Lidl over a cucumber—but he's obviously thinking that this is our first night here and it's best not to start off on the wrong foot. "Now that you're here," he tells Rob, "you can have a look at the leak yourself."

Rob looks like he's about to argue but then acquiesces. "Fine."

"It's this way," Greg says, leading the landlord into our flat. I stay outside on the pretext of folding up the ladder but the truth is, I don't want to go into the flat while Rob is there. Something about him just creeps me out. I'm probably being totally unfair on the poor guy but I can't help what I feel. Best to keep those thoughts to myself though; if Greg learns of my unease, he'll probably expect me to start accusing Rob of kidnapping Amy Donovan or something equally horrendous.

And the worst part is that Greg would be totally justified in thinking that. It's happened before, after all. It would be the Simon Coates case all over again.

Rob comes out of the flat, casts me a glance I can't interpret, and strides away down the hallway to the lift. I take the ladder into the flat to escape his gaze.

Greg is standing in the kitchen, looking up at the water collecting on the ceiling. "He's going to fix it," he tells me. "He's just gone downstairs to get his tools."

"That's all right, then," I say, fixing a smile that I don't really feel onto my face. When we arrived here earlier, I felt so happy but now I just feel hollow inside. How can my mood deteriorate so drastically in just a couple of hours? Maybe it's the storm making me feel this way.

But then a thought hits me and I know that it

isn't the storm at all. Something about what just happened in the hallway doesn't make sense.

Greg looks at me closely. He must see something in my face because he asks, "You okay?"

"Greg, how did he know you were going into the attic?"

He frowns. "Hmm? What do you mean?"

"The landlord. How did he know to come up here and stop you going into the attic?"

Greg thinks about that for a moment and then goes out into the hallway. He points down the hallway towards the lift. "That's how," he says, satisfied that he's solved the mystery.

I peek out and look at what he's pointing at. A small white camera is fixed on the wall above the lift. It points along the hallway towards our front door, its lifeless black eye staring directly at me.

I retreat into the flat. "What's that doing there?"

Greg shrugs. "It's a security camera."

"That means it's watching us."

"That's what security cameras do, Kate."

I pull him into the flat, out of the camera's gaze. "No, I mean *he* was watching us. A security camera recording what happens in a hallway is one thing but he knew you were going into the attic as soon as we got out there which means he must be watching a live feed."

He widens his eyes and puts on a creepy voice. "I bet he has a whole bank of monitors down in the basement and he sits there day and night watching all the tenants as they go about their daily lives."

"Stop it, Greg, it isn't funny." His description frightens me because it's exactly what I've been thinking. Greg is making light of it but I wonder if he's closer to the truth than he realises.

Later, as I lay in bed with Greg snoring beside me, my thoughts return to the incident in the hallway. Something about it still doesn't feel right, even considering the camera in the hallway.

Outside, the storm has abated, the only trace of its passing a strong wind that howls over the moors beyond our bedroom window.

Another noise out there, something other than the wind, alerts my senses. I sit up in bed, listening. I'm sure the sound was the soft *click* of a car door being gently closed. Then I hear an engine start and the crunch of gravel beneath tyres. There is a brief pause and then I hear a car driving away.

I reach for my phone on the bedside table and

check the time. *2:09 a.m.* I should be asleep by now but I have a problem going to sleep in strange places and, for now at least, the flat qualifies as a strange place. Give it a couple of nights and I should be sleeping as soundly as Greg.

Obviously I'm not the only one still awake tonight, though. Sliding out of bed and padding over to the window, I look out and see the rear lights of a car slip into the dark night.

O——

The headlights cut through the night as he takes the road that leads across the moors. The moon, almost full and reflecting off the snow on the ground, makes the moors appear like some ghostly otherworld.

Despite his eagerness to get to his destination, he keeps his speed well below the limit. He can't afford to be stopped by the police, that would be a stupid mistake. When the authorities find his sleeping angel on the moors, they'll cast a net and question anyone who was in this area. It wouldn't do to have a speeding offence on record that places him here. And in the early hours of the morning as well. They'd descend on him like crows on a piece of roadkill. No, that won't do at all.

So he pushes down the anticipation that swells inside his body and forces himself to remain calm. He turns the radio on, realising as he reaches for the button that his hand is shaking. He's waited too long for this. He should have come last night but the police were sniffing around, tramping over the moors in their yellow coats, making him wary.

They were on the moors again today, searching the ground even as the storm raged about them. He wondered if he should stay away from his sleeping angel again tonight but the urge to see her is too strong. Besides, the police are looking in the wrong place; they're days away from finding what they seek.

The slow, heavy pounding of a doom metal song fills the car. The steady funereal rhythm calms him; it's as if the monotonous beat merges with the beating of his heart and slows his organ's pace to that of a dirge.

When he finally reaches his destination, he pulls the car over to the side of the road and kills the engine. He climbs out into the cold night. The savage wind blows over him and he stands with his arms spread and his eyes closed for a few moments, relishing the numbing sensation on his skin. He imagines that he is trapped under ice, in a freezing, watery void. For a couple of seconds, he actually feels that he can't move his limbs and finds himself unable to take a breath for fear that icy water will rush into his lungs.

His eyes snap open and he waits for the feeling to pass. When he can breathe again, he fills his lungs with the dark, bitter night air and moves away from the road, walking through the snow-covered grass and heather towards his sleeping angel. He's leaving footprints that mark his passage but there's another storm coming soon— grey clouds are already collecting over the sea— and a fresh fall of snow will obliterate all trace of him ever being here.

He finds the dip in the land easily and eases himself down the snowy bank to the place where his angel awaits. When he left her here, the natural depression in the landscape was filled with water. Now, the water has frozen and his beauty is encased in ice. This is exactly what he needs.

Dropping to his knees, he uses his hand to wipe snow away from a section of the ice and sees her face, illuminated by the moonlight. She's so beautiful he could cry. So serene. So perfect. Eyes closed, lips slightly parted. Her blonde hair spread about her face like a heavenly halo, accented by the bright red ribbon that he lovingly tied into her golden locks.

Now, he does cry. While the wind and snow whip about him, he looks down at his sleeping angel and weeps with love for her.

## CHAPTER 3

The next morning, I wake to find Greg's side of the bed empty. The sun is beating in through the window and I feel too hot. Throwing the duvet off my body, I climb out of bed and go to the kitchen, where I find a note on the table.

*Didn't want to wake you. Off to new job. Have a good day. See you later. I Love You. Greg xxx*

I grin at the words. Greg is such a softie sometimes and still thoughtful even after seven years of marriage. I hope the first day at his new job goes okay. I feel kind of guilty about it because if it wasn't for me, he'd still be happily working at his old job in Manchester and not starting a new one in Middlesbrough, which is an hour's drive from here.

My therapist told me not to dwell on the past, that what's done is done, but my stupid mistake isn't isolated in the past; it's still affecting us now. Greg is working somewhere new, we're living somewhere else. These things are all down to me. I can't blame anyone else or say it's just the way life goes. My mistake ripped our old life away, tore it up into tiny pieces and let it drift away on the wind like shreds of old newspaper.

I make myself a coffee and take it to my desk, which is situated in the living room, close to the window. My computer fires up as soon as I touch the space bar on the keyboard and I type in the password. There's a folder on here, nested away inside the Documents folder, that is titled *SC*. The innocuous-looking title stands for Simon Coates. The folder contains audio recordings of my interviews with his wife Stella, notes I wrote up while I was investigating Simon, and scans of the newspaper articles that spelled the end of my career as an investigative journalist.

I open the folder, therapist be damned.

The various files appear on the screen and I select a newspaper article from *The Sun*. The headline blares at me.

COATES CLEARED BY POLICE! SAYS HE

WILL SUE FOR DAMAGES AFTER BEING WRONGLY ACCUSED OF MURDER!

The photograph shows Simon Coates leaving a police station in Manchester, flanked by his solicitor and a number of police officers who are holding the press at bay. I was supposed to be there that day, standing among the throng of reporters and photographers outside the station, but I stayed at home and watched the proceedings on TV.

Because, unlike those other members of the press, I was personally involved in the Simon Coates case. I'd written an article that had implied that Simon may have been responsible for the death of his 4-year-old son, Danny.

A week before the photo was taken at the police station, Stella Coates rang me at the Manchester Recorder and said she had a story to tell. I knew who she was from the News, of course. Her son Danny's tragic death had been reported in the papers and on the Internet.

I met Stella in a cafe near the Recorder offices and, as she dabbed at her eyes with a scrunched up piece of tissue, she told me that she thought her husband Simon had murdered Danny.

That surprised me. According to the police

report, the boy had wandered away from his back garden while his father was distracted by a phone call inside the house. The garden backed onto fields that stretched for half a mile before meeting a stream. It was in this stream that Danny's body had been discovered, an hour after he'd gone missing.

According to the police investigation, Danny had simply slipped down the muddy bank and was unable to get out of the stream, which was deep and fast-flowing due to heavy rainfall the night before.

Stella, however, was convinced that Simon had taken the boy to the stream and drowned him there. She told me that Simon hated the boy and often told her how much better their life would be "without kids." She was certain that Danny had been murdered but was afraid to voice her suspicions to the police because her husband was himself a police constable and Stella was afraid the department would close ranks and ignore her. Going to a local newspaper, she thought, would give her a voice.

Looking back at the situation now, I know I should have refused to publish her story. She had no evidence other than her own suspicions and to accuse Simon Coates of murdering his son was libel. I did some perfunctory investigation, asking neighbours if they'd seen anything suspicious and inquiring about the Coates family but I didn't turn up anything that could secure a conviction or even be used in a court of law. A couple of people had seen someone standing by the stream earlier that day but no one could testify it was Simon Coates.

Despite the lack of evidence, I jumped in with both feet and since I was the editor-in-chief of the Manchester Recorder's crime section, as well as the only crime reporter—the paper was small—I was able to get my article into the paper without a senior member of staff using common sense and rejecting it.

I didn't exactly accuse Simon Coates of murder, despite what the headline above the Sun's photo exclaimed. I framed the story as a discussion about unknown causes of death among children and how some mysteries surrounding such deaths might never be solved.

I mentioned a number of cases where foul play might be involved and no one would be any the wiser because of the lack of evidence. One of those cases was the death of Danny Coates. I suggested that perhaps some of these cases should be re-examined.

Despite the Recorder's modest circulation, the story sent shockwaves through the community. Released during a slow news week, it garnered the attention of the national tabloids and soon the headline LOCAL NEWSPAPER ACCUSES SIMON COATES OF MURDERING OWN SON appeared on every newstand and in every newsfeed across the country.

The Recorder, fearing legal action, fired me. It soon became clear that Simon Coates didn't intend to make good on his promise to sue, but not before he threw out a nasty barb on television. A couple of seconds after the photograph had been taken outside the police station, he faced the cameras and said, "Mrs Lumley's own brother died in mysterious circumstances. Perhaps *that* case should be reopened!"

That comment dealt a vicious blow. It left me reeling. I hadn't mentioned Max in my article because I wasn't ready to talk about his death, not even in print. There was a black hole inside me where all of the emotions surrounding my brother's death were hidden and I didn't dare disturb it for fear of what might come flooding out.

I was ten when Max died. Dad told me that there was no one responsible for my brother's death and so I had no one to blame, no one to hate. Unable to express those two emotions, my ten-year-old self had simply placed a mental door over the black hole and locked it.

The only people I ever talked to in any detail about Max were Greg, my best friend Nia, and my therapist. And whenever I spoke of him, it was in a matter-of-fact manner that didn't betray the love I felt for my younger brother, who'd always called me Katy and had an enthusiasm for life.

My therapist, of course, had connected Max to my article about Simon Coates. "Did you write the article because you needed to blame someone for Max's death?" she asked me one afternoon.

"Of course not," I said. "Simon Coates isn't responsible for Max."

"No, he isn't, but your subconscious mind might have felt that finding someone to blame for Danny Coates' death would make up for not finding someone to blame for Max's."

I said nothing.

She continued, peering at me over her glasses. "And that's what you have a hard time accepting;

that sometimes bad things just happen and there's nobody to blame."

I close the folder on the computer and sit back in my chair, letting out a long breath.

Deep down, I know my therapist was right. When I wrote the article for the Recorder, it was Max who had occupied my thoughts and a sense of quiet rage that had fuelled my emotions. I knew that there was no one to blame for Max's death but what if there was someone to blame for Danny's? Didn't the boy deserve justice? If there was even a shadow of a doubt...

Except there wasn't any doubt at all in the police report. Danny's death was ruled accidental and saying otherwise destroyed my career.

Simon Coates might not have sued the Recorder or me but he came after me another way. I started getting phone calls at all hours where the caller would hang up as soon as I answered. On two occasions, I found my tyres slashed. The worst incident was when someone spray-painted the word LIAR over our front door in red paint in the middle of the night.

The harassment went on for months. In the end, Greg decided to apply for a transfer at the bank where he worked. When Middlesbrough became available, he jumped at it because he knew I'd always wanted to live by the sea and it was possible to get a place on the east coast within commuting distance.

My own job, as developmental editor for Wollstonecraft Publishing meant I could work from home, so the change of location wouldn't affect my career.

I down the coffee and get up from the desk. My therapist was right; it's best not to dwell on the past. Thinking about Max makes me feel so helpless, that the world is a cruel place and there's nothing we can do to change it.

After pouring a second mug of coffee, I go to the living room window and look out at the same view I'd fallen in love with yesterday. The landscape has changed since then. The storm clouds that were roiling over the sea have gone, replaced with clear blue sky. The fields and distant cliffs are covered with a white blanket that glitters in the sunshine.

Max would have loved this. When our Mum and Dad took us to the Brecon Beacons in Wales for a holiday of camping and hiking, Max complained that he wanted to go to the seaside instead. He loved the sea. If we'd gone to the sea that year, he would probably still be alive.

In a way, I feel like I've moved here for him. We had good times during our seaside holidays; running along the beach, paddling in the sea, and building sandcastles that would inevitably be washed away by the unstoppable tide. Even though Max was two years younger than me, I never thought of him as the baby of the family; we played together without any care for the age difference between us.

That might have changed eventually if we'd both grown a bit older together but, of course, that never happened. Our relationship froze when I was 10 and he was 8 and we were best friends.

My phone rings, bringing me out of my reverie. It's Nia. She's another reason we decided on Whitby when we were looking for somewhere to live. Nia and her husband live in Robin Hood's Bay, which is only a fifteen minute drive from here.

I've known Nia Mitchell since she was Nia Preston and I was Kate Vance, two teenagers working weekends in a clothing store in Manchester. We both started on the same day and became fast friends. Since then, we've been involved in each other's lives every step of the way. I was Nia's shoulder to cry on when she split up with her first serious boyfriend, and she was mine when Doug Hendrix—a guy I met while working as an apprentice at a local newspaper —and I went our separate ways.

I was maid of honour when Nia married Will and became Nia Mitchell and she was matron of honour when I married Greg four years later. We're godparents to their son and daughter, Jordan and Kishawn, and if Greg and I ever have kids, I'd like Nia and Will to be godparents to them.

As soon as I answer the call and bring the phone to my ear, Nia is already talking.

"Hey, girl, how's it going? Have you settled into your gothic mansion yet?"

I laugh. "As you know, we only rent one floor of said mansion."

"Well that's a start. Anyway, are you too busy unpacking or do you want to meet up for a coffee?"

"Coffee sounds great."

"Okay, do you know a place called Hallowed Grounds? It's on Church Street. We went there a couple of years ago. It's the one where Greg and Will spent most of their time coming up with coffee shop names that were puns."

I groan. "I remember. Has Beans."

"Yeah, that was one of them. Another was Around The Blend."

"We have to make sure they never go into business together."

"So do you remember where it is?"

"Not really," I admit. "But if it's on Church Street, I'll find it."

"Great. I'll see you there in an hour."

An hour isn't much time to get ready but I should be able to make it. "See you then."

"And be careful on the roads," she warns, "there's a lot of ice and snow out there."

"I will."

I hang up and push two pieces of bread into the toaster. After buttering it and eating it at the counter, I take a quick shower, reminding myself to get some mould remover for the tiles while I'm in town, and dress in my warmest clothes. When I check myself in the full-length bedroom mirror, togged up in boots, salopettes, a thick snow jacket and a woollen slouch beanie—from which my blonde hair keeps escaping until I use a hairband to keep it in place beneath the hat—I decide that I look like I'm about trek to Antarctica rather than drive a couple of miles into town.

Still, it'll have to do. I only have twenty minutes left to get into town and find Hallowed Grounds.

I grab the flat key, stuff a pair of fleece-lined gloves into my pockets, and go out into the hallway, locking the door behind me. As I walk beneath the attic hatch, something catches my attention; a shiny silver padlock hanging from a hasp and staple that Rob must have fixed into place. Last night, we heard him walking around in the attic, his footsteps pounding down through our ceiling, and then we heard banging in the hallway. The banging was obviously the sound of him fitting the lock to the attic.

What can he have up there that's so precious? In a house of this age, I'd expect the attic to be full of nothing more than old junk and furniture. I shrug beneath my jacket. Whatever. The attic isn't part of our lease anyway so it's none of my concern, just as long as we don't have any more water leaking into our flat.

I reach the stairs and descend them quickly, relieved that I'm not in the confined space of the lift. And using the stairs should get me to the ground floor in less than the whole minute the lift takes.

When I reach the ground floor—in 45 seconds

if my counting is accurate—Winston appears and starts to rub round my legs, purring. Ivy's door is open and the old lady is sitting at her kitchen table, drinking a cup of tea. I wave in at her and she waves back.

"Good morning, dear. Would you like a cup of tea?"

"I can't right now, I need to get my car defrosted and head into town."

Her face falls slightly. I wonder how many visitors she gets in her flat, if any.

"I'll tell you what," I say. "I'll get the car started and let it run for a while to heat up. While it's doing that, I'd love to have a cup of tea with you."

She brightens and gets up from the table. "I'll put on a fresh pot."

I go outside, being careful not to let Winston follow me, and groan when I see the ice covering the Mini's windscreen and the layer of snow sitting on the roof and bonnet. The day is cold and even though the breeze is nothing like last night's winds, it chills my face as I don the gloves and wipe the snow off the car. I open the driver's door and start the engine, thankful when it purrs into life immediately.

After dialling the heat up to maximum and

turning on the rear windscreen heater, I get out of the car and lock it. That's a precaution I probably don't need to take, since the house is in the middle of nowhere, but city-living and the events of the past year have instilled in me a heightened wariness when it comes to security.

There are two other cars in the parking area, an old green Land Rover Defender and a red Volvo. Like my Mini, each has a layer of snow on its roof and a sheet of ice on its windscreen. But unlike my car, the Land Rover doesn't have any snow on its bonnet. Instead, there is only a pool of water. I remove one glove and go over the car, touching the bonnet. The metal is cold now but it must have been warm when the snow fell early this morning. Was this the car I saw last night from my window?

There's a clear space on the ground, where a parked car shielded the gravel beneath it from the snowfall. It's next to my Mini, where Greg's Honda was parked.

I go back inside to find Winston waiting for me inside the door. He follows me into Ivy's flat where the old lady is sitting at the table again. A pot of tea sits in front of her, along with a set of matching china cups and saucers. There's a pleasant smell of warm biscuits in the kitchen. It's so warm in here, I have to take off my jacket and hat and hang them over the back of my chair before I sit down.

Ivy fills two cups with tea and passes one to me. "Here you are, dear. Might as well start the day right, with a cup of tea." She places a full sugar bowl and cream jug in front of me.

"Thank you," I say. "It's really cold out there."

She nods. "That's why Winston won't go out. He doesn't like the cold. He usually does his business in the garden but when it's like this, he uses his tray instead."

"Have you lived here long?" I ask.

"Twelve years. Since my George died."

"Oh, I'm sorry."

"It was for the best. He was in so much pain from cancer that when the end came, it was a blessing, really. My daughters decided I should live somewhere smaller, easier to manage. Downsizing, they called it." She looks wistfully at her tea cup. "It was all right in the beginning, when I could still get around. But now I have trouble with my hips and I can't get to the bus stop to go into town." She puts her hands up and looks around the flat. "So this is all I have now."

My heart goes out to her. "If you ever want a lift

into town, just let me know. I'll be happy to take you. I'm going there now if you want a lift, or if you want me to bring anything back for you."

"There's no need to trouble yourself, dear."

"It's no trouble, really."

She looks pensively at the window. "Well, I wouldn't want to go out in this weather but perhaps some other time. That's very kind of you." She reaches forward and taps my hand with her icy fingers. "Now, you must have a biscuit. I baked them this morning so they're still nice and warm." She gets up, opens one of the kitchen cupboards, and brings out a plate of shortbread biscuits. Setting the plate down on the table between us, she gestures to them. "Help yourself, dear."

Despite having recently eaten two slices of toast, I gratefully pick up a biscuit and take a bite. It's wonderfully warm, with a delicious buttery taste. "These are amazing!"

Ivy beams. "I'll wrap some up for you so you can take them home and give some to your husband. He was telling me this morning how good they smelled while they were baking."

"You saw Greg this morning?"

"Yes, he's a lovely chap. You've done all right for yourself with that one." She winks at me and takes the biscuits to the counter, where she puts half a dozen of them into a small Tupperware container and snaps the lid shut.

When she brings the container back to the table, I say, "I suppose you see everyone who comes and goes, being here on the ground floor."

Ivy nods sagely. "Nothing much gets past me."

"I heard a car last night. Well, this morning, really—"

"Just after two this morning," she says. She points out of the open front door. "It was him. He goes out at all hours of the night. Thinks I don't know about it but I sleep as light as a feather. If a mouse sneezed on the second floor, I'd hear it. And his car's noisy."

"Is it the green one?"

She nods. "The Land Rover."

"Where do you think he goes at that time of night?" I ask lightly.

"I don't know." She looks at me closely and lowers her voice. "It all seems a bit sinister to me."

"Sinister?" I wonder if Ivy knows something about Rob or if she's just making up a story to entertain me.

"I have my suspicions," she says, tapping her

nose and winking at me. "I think he gets up to all sorts."

I lean closer and whisper conspiratorially, hoping she'll elaborate. "Like what?"

She pauses momentarily, probably for dramatic effect, before whispering, "Nightclubs."

"Nightclubs?"

Sitting back in her chair, Ivy nods and takes a sip of her tea. "They get up to all kinds of things in those places. Drugs for one thing. I wouldn't put it past him. He seems spaced out most of the time."

Her answer disappoints me. I thought she might have some real suspicions regarding Rob; something I—

*I could what? Investigate? Those days are gone, Kate. You have a good job, a good husband, and a nice flat by the sea. You don't want to rock the boat.*

I finish my tea and biscuit and thank Ivy. "Now, I really must be going. Is there anything you want me to bring you back from town?"

"No, I'm fine, dear. You have a nice time."

When I get into the Mini, most of the ice has melted off the windscreen, leaving streaks of water on the glass. The wipers are still frozen so I get out of the car again and use my glove to dry the windscreen.

As I do, I notice that someone else has been out here recently. A fresh set of boot prints leads from around the rear of the house to my Mini. I'm sure the prints weren't there when I came out to start the car and closer inspection shows me that they lead right to up my driver's door.

They don't go to any other vehicle; not to the Land Rover or the Volvo. Only the Mini.

Did someone try to get into my car while I was having tea with Ivy?

I follow the prints back around the rear of the house. There's a small garden back here, covered with snow, and a flagstone path that follows the edge of the house to a door. That's where the footprints begin, just outside the door.

The door itself is fairly innocuous looking: heavy wood painted black with a large brass door knob. I wonder if this is Northmoor House's original back door. It probably led into a kitchen in Victorian times. But where does it lead now?

I grasp the knob and push but the door is firmly locked.

It doesn't take much mental calculation to figure out who came out of this door and went to my car. Rob North.

I walk back to my car and climb in, checking

that nothing is missing from the glove box even though there's nothing of value in there anyway and the car was locked. I also check the back seat.

Satisfied that no one actually got inside, I put the car into gear, gently press the accelerator, and ease out of my parking space and through the open gate in the low stone wall that surrounds the Northmoor House.

When I get the car onto the snowy road and trundle slowly past the house to make sure I don't slide into said wall, I happen to glance at the basement window.

As I look, a shadow moves away from the window and melts into the darkness within.

# CHAPTER 4

"You found it!" Nia says, getting up from a table as I enter Hallowed Grounds. Despite the weather, the coffee shop is full of people. There's a smell of roast coffee beans drifting from the kitchen and the place is full of sound: customers chattering, cups and saucers clattering, and the clanging of forks on plates. As well as coffee, Hallowed Grounds serves cakes and most people seem to have a slice of chocolate cake or strawberry gateau on the table in front of them.

Nia hugs me and guides me to a table in the corner. "Haven't seen you in a while. You're looking good."

I smile at her compliment, even though I feel as if the move has aged me a couple of years. I've noticed new wrinkles around my eyes and I'm sure I look much worse-for-wear than the last time I met Nia. She, on the other hand, really doesn't look as if she's aged a day.

We order coffee and chocolate cake and while we're waiting for it to arrive at our table, I tell Nia about our run-in with Rob North and the new lock on the attic.

"Wow, he sounds weird," she says. "Remember when we lived in that flat in Manchester and the landlord was a real creep?"

"I remember he seemed to have a thing for you," I tell her.

Our order arrives and Nia takes a forkful of chocolate cake. Before she eats it, she says, "I bet he couldn't believe his luck the day we moved in there. A red hot black girl and a curvy blonde. It was probably his greatest lesbian fantasy come true."

I laugh. "Yeah, he did seem to think we were a couple. Hey, how come in that description, you're red hot and I'm just curvy? Is that what you think of me? I'm not hot like you?"

She shrugs and looks at me innocently. "I'm just saying what *he* thought. I can't help how his mind worked." She pops the forkful of cake into her mouth and grins.

I shoot an incredulous look at her and sip my coffee, looking out of the condensation-covered window at the passersby walking along Church Street. The street itself is quaint and cobbled, winding from the main road to the foot of the steps that lead up to a 12th Century church and the ruins of Whitby Abbey.

*This is my home now*, I remind myself. *I'm going to be happy here.*

"Did you hear the news this morning?" Nia asks, solemn now.

"No, I've been rushing around. What happened?"

"The police are saying they think that girl that went missing is dead," she says. "They're searching for a body now."

"Amy Donovan?"

She nods. "They found those other two bodies on the moors last year, so that's where they're looking now."

"Yeah, they're searching behind our flats. Do they think she was a victim of the Snow Killer?" Last year, two young women had been abducted from their homes and later found on the moors in the dead of winter. The year before that, one woman had disappeared on New Year's Day and had been found on the moors three days later. The media had dubbed the murderer the Snow Killer, because the each victim went missing during a snowstorm.

Some news outlets preferred the name Red Ribbon Killer because there was a rumour—unsubstantiated by the police—that each of the victims had been found with a red ribbon tied in her hair.

"Snow Killer, Red Ribbon Killer, whatever you want to call him," Mia says. "That guy. He took two women last year, one the year before. So what will it be this year? Three? I'm sensing a pattern here." She looks out of the window and shivers, as if she's seen the killer peering in at us from the street.

"You need to be careful," she tells me, picking up another forkful of chocolate cake and waving it in my direction. "All of those women were blondes."

"But none of them disappeared from Whitby,"

"They were all from this area," Nia says. "The village where Amy Donovan lived is only a few miles away."

"I'll be careful," I tell her. "I'm always careful,

especially after the harassment we endured last year."

"Well, it's a good thing you moved," she says. "I was out of my mind with worry while you were living there." Her face brightens and she grins, adding, "And now you're closer to us. You and Greg must come round for dinner one evening. The kids are dying to see you."

"Of course," I say. "Just let me know when and we'll be there."

"I'll check my calendar and send you a few dates. I'll have to check the kids' calendars as well; with all their sleepovers and after-school activities, they have a busier social life than me and Will."

"I find that hard to believe; you and Will always used to be going out, even after you had Jordan and Kishawn."

"Not anymore," she says. "We've settled down." She pauses and then adds, "Well, settled into a rut might be more appropriate."

"Anything you want to talk about?"

She shrugs. "There's nothing in particular that's changed, we just seem to have grown apart a bit. I don't know, it's hard to explain. It feels like the spark's gone."

"After eleven years of marriage, you can't expect it to be like it was when you first met."

"I know that. Of course I know that. But sometimes, Will seems distant, like he just doesn't care anymore. And the worse thing is, I don't care that he doesn't care. Does that make sense?"

"Sounds like you need a weekend away, just the two of you. Maybe rekindle the spark."

"Maybe," she says. "But who'd look after the kids?"

"Look no further," I say. "Greg and I would be happy to have them for a weekend."

Now it's her turn to look incredulous. "Are you sure?"

"They can come and stay at the flat. We had them that time you and Will went to his brother's funeral, remember?"

"Yeah, but Kishawn was only three then, a little angel. Now she's nine and an unholy terror. And Jordan's seven. So as you can imagine, they fight like cats and dogs all the time."

"I'm sure they'd be well-behaved. Anyway, have a think about it and let me know. The offer stands."

"Thanks, Kate." She takes a gulp of coffee and sets the mug down with a satisfied sigh. "How are things with you and Greg? It can't have been easy with all that trouble you went through."

I think about that for a moment. Greg and I had a couple of full-blown arguments—mainly about why I published the article incriminating Simon Coates—but then we seemed to pull together. And when our home was under attack, the bond between us became even stronger as we tried to protect ourselves from a common enemy. In fact, our marriage has never been better. But I don't feel like telling Nia that if she's having problems in her own marriage. Too much like rubbing it in.

"We're fine," I say. "We haven't really had time to fall into a rut with everything that's been going on."

"Maybe I need to get myself a stalker."

I shake my head, recalling the months of harassment, the feeling of being watched everywhere I went, the sense of danger that loomed over me all the time. "No," I say. "Believe me, you don't want that."

We finish our drinks and order a second round. I opt for tea this time, aware of how much caffeine I've consumed already today. The conversation turns to lighter subjects, such as the amount of homework Jordan and Kishawn bring home every day, Nia's job as an accountant for a firm in Scarborough, and Kishawn's music lessons (she's learning violin) and aspirations to play in an orchestra.

By the time we finish a third round of drinks (tea again for me, although now I know I'm going to be spending most of the day on the loo), we've caught up with each other's lives and reaffirmed the bond between us. We hug on the street outside Hallow Grounds before Nia heads off to her car and I decide to explore the shops.

After browsing the windows of the various gift shops and jewellery shops featuring pieces fashioned from Whitby jet, a pure black gemstone local to the area, I make my way back along Church Street. I go into the Whitby Bookshop and buy the new Val McDermid and an older John Grisham before wandering over the bridge and ambling along the road towards the pier. Even in early January, the seaside town is bustling with people, especially along the Pier Road where the noise and lights of the Amusements attract customers with promises of prizes from the claw grabbers and slot machines.

The beach is less busy and I walk along it for a

while, listening to the incoming tide rolling over the pebbles and sand as I saunter beneath the West Cliff. I imagine what it will be like here in summer, when the beach will be full of children running around with buckets and spades, making sandcastles and playing in the sea.

Just like our family holidays when Mum and Dad took us to Blackpool or Bournemouth. When Max and I felt like we could do anything, even defy the tide to wash our sandcastles away. It always did, of course, but we were full of optimism as we built ever taller and larger structures, only to watch them get washed away with a sense of disappointment and awe.

I gaze along the shoreline and imagine Max splashing through the shallow water, laughing with pure glee. He would have loved it here.

That thought fills me with sadness and I decide to head home.

The walk back to the car, which is parked by the Railway Station, takes me back long Pier Road, which is noisy with the sound of seagulls hovering over the harbour, waiting for the fishing boats to come in, and bright as the sun reflects off the water ice on the pavement where the ice has melted.

It's getting warmer now, and when I reach the

car, I throw my jacket and hat into the boot before sliding into the driver's seat. Checking my phone, I see that I have two missed calls: one from my parents and one from Helen, my therapist. Helen is probably calling to confirm our appointment next week. I thought I was going to have to stop seeing her when I moved to Whitby—the drive to Manchester is just too far—but she suggested we continue our appointments online via video calls.

I decide to ring Helen back first. Confirming the appointment will take a couple of minutes whereas talking to Mum and Dad could go on for a while.

Her phone rings and rings until it goes to an answering machine. I decide to leave a message even though I hate talking to machines. "Hi, Helen, it's Kate Lumley. You rang me earlier and I'm just returning your—"

"Kate," she says, picking up. "I'm here. I was just ringing to make sure you're okay."

"Yes, I'm fine" I say, wondering why I deserve this special treatment. Helen has never rung me to see how I am before.

"Oh," she says on the other end of the line. "You haven't heard, have you?"

"Heard what?"

"Well, perhaps it's best if you hear it from me rather than the news."

"What's happened?" I ask, worried now.

"It's Stella Coates," Helen says. "She's been taken into custody."

"What? What for?"

"She killed her husband. Simon Coates is dead."

## CHAPTER 5

I'm not sure how to process that information. Why would Stella do such a thing? I know why, of course; she thinks Simon killed their son. But why would she throw her life away like that? She'll probably spend the rest of it behind bars. That isn't what Danny would have wanted for his mother.

"Kate, are you still there?"

"Yes, I'm here. I just can't believe she'd do that." I feel shocked, in a daze.

"Listen," she says, "If you want to move your appointment forward, I have some free time tomorrow morning—"

"No, that's fine," I say. I can't run to my therapist every time something bad happens. My appointment can wait until next week. My thoughts keep returning to poor Stella. She must be in a police cell right now, uncertain of her future.

"Are you sure you're all right?" .

"Yes, I'm fine. Thanks for ringing. I'll talk to you next week." I end the call and sit looking out of the car window for a while. Around me, people go about their lives as usual. Popping into the Co Op next to the car park to get food for their families. Standing on the pavement chatting about the weather. Eating fish and chips as they stroll along the road.

I get out of the car, needing some air, and stand there leaning on the bonnet for a few minutes. I don't even know if Simon Coates was a killer, as Stella claimed, or if she's murdered an innocent man. I need to know how it happened. Simon and Stella split up after Danny's death, so how did they meet up for the final time? Did Stella track him down and kill him or was she acting in self defence?

I search the News app on my phone and find a story entitled WIFE KILLS HUSBAND SHE ACCUSED OF MURDER just below the top story of the day: POLICE DOUBT AMY DONOVAN STILL ALIVE.

The story on Stella doesn't offer much information, only that she was arrested at her home after calling the police herself and saying that she'd killed her husband. The police found Simon's body in the same stream where Danny had been discovered. Simon had been stabbed repeatedly with a pair of kitchen scissors which were also found in the stream. The article also mentioned that today would have been Danny Coates's fifth birthday.

I turn the phone off and go into the Co Op, grabbing a basket as I walk through the automatic doors. I buy some essentials, like bread and milk, and enough groceries to get us through the week. I also pick up a tin of tuna for Winston. The mindless task of shopping helps me deal with the numbness I feel regarding Stella Coates. It doesn't take my mind off the situation but gives it more familiar things to deal with, like choosing between two different brands of ham.

I drive back to Northmoor House carefully, especially when I hit the road that winds along the edge of the moors to the house. In town, the snow on the roads has been reduced to muddy slush by passing vehicles and pedestrians but out here, it's still thick and white and untouched.

I unload the shopping bags from the car and head inside Northmoor House, deciding not to use the rickety lift. Ivy's door is closed and so is Rob's as I hurry past it. At the foot of the stairs, I gather the shopping bags into a tight grip in both hands and begin my ascent. Halfway up the first flight, I realise I should have made two trips. By the time I reach the first floor landing, I'm huffing and puffing and wondering if I should have made a New Year's resolution to join a gym.

I drop half the bags and continue up the stairs with a considerably lighter load. Once I get these bags upstairs, I'll go back down for the others.

After dropping the first load by the flat door, I turn and go back to the top of the stairs. But before I can go back down to the first floor, I see a young man coming up, carrying my shopping bags.

He sees me and smiles. "I think you forgot these."

"I was just coming down to get them," I tell him.

"No problem, let's get them to your door." He deposits the bags alongside the others and says, "I'm Mike, by the way. I live on the first floor." He holds out his hand.

We shake and I thank him for his help. He has

a kind, open face, blue eyes, and fair hair. A close-cropped beard makes him look maybe a little older than he actually is, which I guess to be mid-twenties. He's smartly dressed in a black crew neck jumper with a white shirt beneath it and dark blue jeans.

"I'm Kate," I say. "My husband and I moved in yesterday."

"Yes, I met Greg this morning, out in the car park. We had a bit of a chat while we were de-icing our cars. Anyway, I'll let you get on. Nice to meet you." He gives me a little wave and walks back to the stairs.

"You too," I say as I fumble my key out of my pocket and open the door. I slide the shopping bags inside one-by-one and close the door again, leaning on it for a minute while I get my breath back. Next time I go shopping, I'm going to have to use the lift, no matter how slow it is.

I put the groceries into the kitchen cupboards and the fridge, wondering if I might make something for tea. Greg usually does all the cooking, says he loves it. No matter how long a day he's had at work, he likes to spend time in the kitchen, unwinding while he cooks. And his dishes are amazing so who am I to keep him from doing what he loves?

After everything is put away, I treat myself to one of Ivy's shortbread biscuits and take a seat at my desk. I need to get some work done. My current project is a Gothic Romance book called *The Secrets of Falcon House*, a tale of love and peril set in Cornwall in the 1800s. The description that the author sent to Wollstonecraft Publishing ends with the line: *What secrets lie hidden in Falcon House?*

*What secrets lie hidden in* Northmoor *House?* I wonder. *What monstrosity is hidden in the attic, secured by lock and key?* I look up at the ceiling above my head. Maybe if I knock on it, someone will knock in response. Perhaps there's someone locked up there; a modern day Mrs Rochester.

Telling myself to stop being silly and focus on the task at hand, I read through a couple of chapters of Falcon House, correcting the author's typos here and there and making notes where I feel the story could be improved.

Overall, it's a good story and when I finally decide to take a break, three hours have slipped by. I sit back in the chair and rub my eyes. Outside, it's beginning to get dark.

Remembering the tin of tuna I got for

Winston, I grab it off the counter and take it downstairs. It's obvious that Ivy is lonely and isolated here in the house. It seems as if her daughters put her here and then forgot about her. The tuna is an excuse to go and knock on her door without Ivy thinking I'm checking up on her. My grandmother was a very proud woman who wouldn't accept charity or pity from anyone and I get the feeling Ivy is the same.

If I bought something for *her* from the shop, she'd probably refuse it, but something for her *cat* is a different matter.

When I get to the ground floor, I notice that Rob North's door is open but he doesn't seem to be around. I slow my pace as I pass the open door and look in. A flight of steps leads down to another door, which is also open. All I can see down there is a section of ratty green carpet. I'm almost curious enough to go down a few steps so I can see more but I have no idea if Rob is down there or if he'll appear in the hallway and catch me intruding.

So instead of sneaking into the basement flat, I knock on Ivy's door. I hear the old lady's voice talking to Winston and then the door opens.

"Hello, dear," Ivy says, her face brightening

when she sees me. "Come in and I'll make us a cup of tea."

"Thanks," I say, going in and shutting the door behind me. "I brought a tin of tuna for Winston."

"Oh, bless you. He'll like that, won't you boy?" This question is asked of the cat, who rubs around her legs as she makes her way to the kitchen. I follow her, then stop at the door when I see Rob North lying on his back on the kitchen floor, head inside the cupboard under Ivy's sink. There's a large open toolbox next to his legs, his baseball cap resting on top of it.

Ivy must sense my hesitation because she waves me into the kitchen. "It's all right, dear, he's just fixing a leak under my sink. I reported it a week ago and he's finally got around to doing something about it." She emphasises the word "finally" and aims her words at Rob's torso and legs.

"I've been busy," he says, his voice muffled by the fact that his head is in the cupboard.

"Busy my backside," Ivy retorts. She clicks the kettle on and waits, arms folded, for it to boil. As she does so, she scowls down at Rob.

I also look at him and see that where his T-shirt has ridden up, wicked-looking scars are visible on his stomach and sides. It looks like his body is covered in them.

I avert my gaze as he slides out from within the cupboard and gets to his feet. "All fixed," he says to Ivy. He hasn't acknowledged my presence here at all. When I finally look at him, I notice a long scar stretching from just above his temple to the back of his head. He sees me staring and fixes the baseball cap onto his head.

"Good," Ivy says. "Next time, respond a bit earlier. I can't have water leaking out from my cupboard. Winston was drinking it. What if it's poisonous?"

He sighs. "It's the same water that comes out of the tap." He packs up his tools and hefts the toolbox before stepping past me and into the living room. He opens the front door and exits without another word.

"Bye then," Ivy shouts after him. She turns to me, shaking her head. "That boy has no manners. No manners at all."

"Do you know where he got those scars?" I ask as she fusses with the teapot and cups.

"What's that, dear? Oh, yes, I think he must have got those from the accident." She drops some teabags into the pot and adds water from the kettle.

"The accident?"

"The car accident." She closes the lid on the pot and turns to face me. "Apparently, it was quite awful. The whole family was involved. It didn't happen here, though. They were on holiday at the time."

"That sounds terrible."

She nods, then frowns, as if racking her brain for some information. "Were they in Spain? No, that's where Fred and Wanda live now. Oh, I can't remember, dear. I'm not very good with names and places."

"Don't worry about it," I say. The fact that Ivy constantly calls me "dear" has already made me suspect that she can't remember my name.

"Now you sit down and I'll bring the tea," she says.

I sit at the kitchen table and she brings the china tea set over and pours a drink for both of us. "Would you like a biscuit?" she asks.

"No, thank you, I really couldn't. I've had enough cake and biscuits today to sink a battleship. I won't be able to eat my dinner."

She puts sugar and milk into her tea and stirs it thoughtfully. "I've been thinking about what I told you this morning," she says. "About me not being able to get out. Now, I don't want you thinking that I'm a helpless old lady stuck in this flat. I have my groceries delivered, and my newspaper every day. And my daughters visit me every now and then. I do all right. And when the weather's nice, I go out in the garden."

"I don't think you're helpless at all," I assure her.

"Good."

"Do you know where that door leads to? The one in the garden."

Her eyebrows knit together for a moment as she considers this. "I don't think it leads anywhere, dear. I suppose it was the original back door, back when the house was a single dwelling. Now that it's been separated into flats, I can't think where that door would lead to. There's probably nothing behind it but a brick wall."

I know that isn't the case; someone stepped out of that door this morning and walked around the house to my car. But it's obvious Ivy doesn't know anything about it so I change the subject. "What are your daughters' names?"

"Chloe and Laura," she says. "They're both

married. Chloe has a son." She thinks for a moment. "Sam. Yes, that's it: Sam."

"Does he visit you?"

Her eyes turn sad. "He's been here once or twice but I haven't seen him in a long time."

"Oh, I'm sorry."

"Don't be. It isn't your fault. And you're here keeping me company so don't apologise for my daughters. You're a much kinder person than they are; I knew that as soon as I met you."

I feel a well of pity for Ivy and a tinge of dislike for her daughters. No matter how busy they are with their own lives, they should make time for their mother. She won't be around forever and they've forgotten her already. Then I feel a stab of guilt when I remember that I haven't called my parents back yet.

Changing the subject to something that won't make Ivy feel down, I ask, "What do you like to watch on the telly?"

"This and that. Anything that keeps me amused. Oh, you just reminded me, it's almost time for *Neighbours*." She gets up and shuffles over to the sofa, picking up a remote from the side table as she sits down. She points it at the TV and flicks it as if it's a wand as she presses the button to turn the telly on. "Are you going to watch it with me?" she asks as the theme music begins.

"Sure," I say, joining her on the sofa. Winston jumps up and sits between us. As the programme goes on, I have no idea what's happening or who the characters are but Ivy seems happy to have some company. Winston closes his eyes and settles down for a nap.

When the closing credits come on half an hour later, Ivy says, "It's *Home & Away* next. Are you going to stay for that?"

"I think I should get back to my own flat," I tell her. There's something I want to do before Greg gets home.

Ivy looks disappointed but nods. "All right, dear. Mind how you go."

I let myself out of her flat but instead of heading for the stairs, I go outside and walk around to the rear of the building. The snow has almost all gone now, melted away as if it were never here.

Starting at the corner of the house, I walk along the path to the mysterious door, counting my strides as I do so. Forty five.

Then I go back inside and count out the same number of strides along the hallway, beginning at

the entrance door. That take me past Ivy's and
Rob's doors, almost to the staircase. But not quite. I
turn to my left, the direction of the rear of the
house, and face a blank wall. Behind this wall is
the room the back door leads to. Unless it's been
bricked up as Ivy suggested.

I put my ear close to the wall and rap on it
three times with my knuckles. It sounds hollow.
There's a room back there that seemingly can only
be reached by the black door that opens onto the
garden.

*It's probably just where Rob keeps the lawnmower
and gardening tools*, I tell myself. But I know that's
unlikely; I've already seen the large shed at the
bottom of the garden. Surely the garden tools are
kept in there.

To satisfy my curiosity, I go back outside and
wander down the garden, pretending I'm just
having a look around. For all I know, Rob could be
watching me from one of the windows in the
house. "And speaking of windows," I murmur to
myself as my gaze travels up to the roof high above
me, "there's a window in the attic." A small dormer
window juts out from the roof like a dark eye
staring down at me.

I turn away from the house and resume my

walk along the lawn, pretending to inspect the trees and shrubs while I try to look at the shed out of the corner of my eye. A padlock secures the door but I can see in through the window.

I was right; there are tools in there, including a lawn mower. Whatever the room behind the back door is, it isn't a storeroom for gardening equipment.

I go back inside and up to the second floor. As I pass beneath the large attic hatch, which Greg said tilted down like a ramp and might even have stairs built into it, I wonder if anyone ever lived up there. The dormer window suggests it could be a possibility. Maybe my imagined Mrs Rochester character isn't so far from the truth after all.

Or maybe the hatch is wider and longer than usual simply so that large items of furniture can be stored in the attic.

See, there's a simple explanation for everything.

I enter the flat and close the door before leaning back on it and taking stock of my new home.

The flat was supposed be perfect; close to the sea, in a lovely Victorian building, away from our past troubles. Nothing has changed; it still has all those things going for it and it *is* perfect. But something has changed in my outlook. Why am I looking for things that don't seem right about the house?

So what if I don't know what's in the room behind the back door? It's really nothing to do with me. I'm just being nosy.

So what if the landlord is rude? There are lots of rude people in the world. Judging by his behaviour in Ivy's flat, Rob seems to want to ignore me and that's fine by me.

So what if an unknown person walked out of that door and went to my car? Maybe they were just wondering why the Mini's engine was running with no one inside.

I shouldn't let these things bother me.

Yet they do.

When I worked as an investigative journalist, Greg said my mind was always in work mode, trying to unravel things and place them into a sensible pattern. I don't like unknowns. As far as I'm concerned, mysteries should be solved, secrets uncovered.

According to Mum, my inquisitive mindset began right after Max died. Because I don't know *for sure, without a shadow of doubt*, what happened.

The police, the coroner, and my parents are satisfied that Max wandered away from our campsite and fell into a ravine but no one can say with any certainty if that is *exactly* what happened. What if someone took him from the campsite and left him to wander in the wilderness? What if someone pushed him to his death?

Unanswered questions. I can't stand them.

Knowing that I'll never know exactly what happened to my little brother, I decide to get a couple of hours of work done. If I can't solve the mysteries of Northmoor House, maybe I can read how the ones in Falcon House turn out.

It's almost an hour later, as I'm sitting at my desk, that I hear a noise above my head. At first, I'm sure I must be mistaken. The heroine in Falcon House is about to discover what her husband has hidden in the folly and I've been with her every step of the way as she creeps through the moonlit garden to the dark structure. The noise I heard is surely nothing more than the result of my overactive imagination, fuelled by the tense scene in the book.

But then I hear it again, soft footfalls above my head. Someone is in the attic, walking around up there but trying to be quiet.

Spinning my chair away from the desk and pushing myself out of it, I rush out of the flat and into the hallway, expecting the ramp to be down and for the mystery of the attic to be solved once and for all. Maybe I can get a look in there and satisfy my curiosity.

But the hatch is closed and locked, the silver padlock dangling from the hasp.

No, that can't be right. I wasn't hearing things. I know there's someone up there.

I pivot back into the flat and stand stock still in the middle of the living room, listening. The footsteps are still moving about in the attic, the floorboards up there creaking under someone's weight.

Outside, I hear a car crunching over the gravel. I go to the window and see Greg's silver Honda pull into the space next to my Mini. He gets out and crosses to the door, briefcase in hand.

The ceiling continues creaking as someone passes over it.

When Greg appears at the doorway, he looks at me with a bemused expression on his face. "What are you up to?"

"Ssshh. Listen." I point up at the ceiling.

Greg looks up and listens for a moment, then

looks back at me and shrugs. "What am I listening to?"

"Someone's in the attic," I whisper.

This prompts a second shrug, a lengthier one this time, accompanied by arched eyebrows. "So?"

"What are they doing up there?"

"Hopefully checking for more leaks."

"Look at the attic hatch."

He leans out of the door and looks along the hallway. "It's closed. And still locked."

"So how is someone up there?"

"Kate, there's probably another way up. I don't see what the problem is. You weren't like this last night when Rob was stomping around up there."

"This is different," I tell him. "Like you just said, Rob was stomping around last night. We knew he was up there fixing the leak. This time we don't know what he's doing up there. And he's...creeping."

Greg puts his briefcase down and closes the door to the hallway. "Creeping? Now you sound paranoid. He has a right to go into his own attic and creep or stomp as the mood takes him. He can even dance up there is he wants." He laughs at his own attempt at humour.

"This isn't funny." I know that technically, Greg

is right; Rob can go into the attic by whatever secret route he pleases. In fact, now that I think about it, we didn't actually see him go up there last night so he might have used the same unseen access point he's using now instead of the hatch in the hallway.

But remembering those furtive footsteps directly above my head is still making me feel creeped out, despite Greg's logical assessment of the situation.

"See?" Greg says, "he's gone now."

I listen carefully, straining my ears to hear the slightest sound that would betray Rob's presence in the space above our heads. There's nothing. It's gone quiet up there.

"Right," Greg says. "I'm going to make some food. I'm starving. How does spaghetti sound?"

"Great," I say, following him into the kitchen. "How was your first day?"

"It was good. The work is basically the same as I did in Manchester but now I'm doing it with a lot of new people. A few of them took me to lunch to welcome me into the fold."

"I bet you loved that." Greg loves meeting new people and being in their company. I'm sure his name is short for gregarious. I'm the opposite; I have a few close friends I can trust and that's it. Quality over quantity.

"It was fun," he says, retrieving the frying pan and a saucepan from the cupboard. "I think I'm going to like it there. My boss, Terry, seems to be a nice guy and the other managers are very friendly."

I'm relieved to hear that. If Greg didn't like his new job, I'd feel totally responsible. "I bought a bottle of wine to celebrate."

"Great, I'll put some into the bolognese as well."

I lean against the kitchen table and watch him as he makes dinner. Even after being together for nine years—seven of them married—I love watching Greg cook. He becomes totally focused on the task at hand, precise in the way he adds ingredients to the pan, and I can sense an enthusiasm in him that comes from knowing he's good at what he does and knowing the result will be mouth-wateringly delicious.

Soon, the kitchen is filled with the smell of garlic, tomatoes, and basil. The meat sizzles in the frying pan and the salted water for the pasta bubbles in the saucepan. I'm suddenly so hungry that I can barely wait for Greg to dish the meal out.

"Did you hear the news?" I ask him when we finally sit down at the table, the dishes of spaghetti and two glasses of red wine between us. "About Stella Coates?"

He nods. "Sounds like she finally flipped."

"You make her sound like she had mental issues."

He takes a sip of wine. "Her actions made it obvious that she did, don't they?"

"Greg, she thought Simon killed their child."

"But he didn't." Before I can protest, he raises a hand and adds, "Not in any way that can be proven."

"Just because it can't be proven doesn't mean he didn't do it."

"In the eyes of the law it does. The only evidence was circumstantial. And now Stella is going to be spending the rest of her life in prison."

I take a few bites of spaghetti and then say, "I think I should visit her."

Greg looks at me incredulously. "What? Why?"

"I feel partly responsible. It was my story that blew everything up. Maybe if I hadn't published it—"

"Kate, no. Listen to me. Publishing the story was a mistake, we all know that, but everything you wrote came out of Stella's mouth. They were her words, not yours. You are in no way responsible for her murdering Simon."

"I know that, it's just—" I let my words trail off. I can't explain how I feel. I spoke with Stella on lots of occasions after her son's death. She was confused and distraught, seeking answers that might never be found. I tried to help her but only made things worse, both for herself and me. It felt like we were the only two people in the world who suspected there might be more to Danny's death than the official verdict. Now that Stella's in prison, how alone must she be feeling? I need to let her know that I haven't abandoned her.

"I hope this isn't some sort of guilt you're feeling," Greg says. "If you did anything wrong, then you more than paid for it by having to endure over a year's worth of harassment. We both did."

"I'm sorry," I say. "I had no idea it was going to get ugly like that."

"You have nothing to apologise for. You did what you thought was right at the time." He takes another sip of wine and brightens. "Hey, we're here now, in our new home. By the sea. I'd say things worked out all right in the end, wouldn't you?"

I nod and spin my fork in my spaghetti, wrapping it with pasta.

"How was your day?" Greg asks. "Did you do some more work on that heroine in peril story?"

"*The Secrets of Falcon House*," I say. "Yes, I did a couple of hours on it. And I went into town to meet Nia."

"Aha!" He points his fork at me. "I thought it wouldn't take you two long to get together now we've moved up here."

"It was nice to see her again. We had a coffee at that place we went to the last time we visited them."

"That place with the funny name."

"Hallowed Grounds."

He grins. "Ah yes, I remember. Will and I were coming up with similar names for coffee shops."

"Has Beans," I remind him.

"Yes, that was one of mine."

We spend the rest of the meal reminiscing about about the various times we visited Nia and Will. I don't tell him that Nia thinks their marriage may be in trouble. I hope it's just a blip that will sort itself out.

Later, as I lie in bed awake while Greg sleeps softly next to me. I hear footsteps on the gravel outside and a car door opening. Then an engine starts and idles for a second or two before I hear the car roll over the gravel and out onto the road. As the car drives away and the sound fades into the distance, I check the time on my bedside clock. *1:30.*

I tell myself that I'm going to stay awake and see what time the car returns. But half an hour later, I drift into a sleep where I dream of Max.

# CHAPTER 6

*July 26th, 1992*

"We're all going on a summer holiday," Dad sings as we drive along the motorway to Wales. Mum looks back at me and Max and rolls her eyes but I know she's only joking. She likes Dad's singing really and she likes it when he's being silly, like he is now, singing an old song that only he and Mum know.

Max and I are sitting in the back of the car. I'm a bit excited to be going camping but Max is a bit sulky because he wanted to go to the seaside. I don't blame him really because I like the seaside as well but camping sounds fun and Dad says there are mountains in Wales. They're not as high as Mount Everest, which I learned about in Geography, but they're really high.

And we get to sleep in a tent, which is something we don't do when we go to the seaside. We stay in a caravan usually. Or sometimes a chalet in a holiday resort which is nice because I usually make friends with other children who are also on holiday and we play together on the beach while our parents sit on deck chairs and shout at us to put sun cream on.

When I make friends with other children, I always let Max play with us as well. I'm his older sister so I have to look after him. Besides, he's lots of fun. Always happy and running about. The other children usually don't mind that he's with us, even though he's younger than us.

"Come on, you three, sing along," Dad says.

"We don't know your old songs," I tell him.

"Katy," Max says, pulling on the sleeve of my cardigan. "You won't climb the mountain too fast and leave me behind, will you?"

"Of course not, silly. Why do you say that?"

He shrugs and looks out of his window at the the cars going past us. "I don't think I'll be very good at climbing mountains."

"Of course you will," Mum says. "And besides, the mountains we're going to aren't so steep that you have to climb them like the mountaineers on telly. We'll just be walking up them. So there's no need to worry, Max."

He nods but doesn't say anything. I don't know why he isn't his usual funny self today.

---

The campsite is right at the foot of the mountain. While Mum and Dad put the tent up, Max and I go exploring. There's a shop on the campsite that mostly sells food but they do have some footballs and frisbees in the window. And there are lots of other tents with families in them. So there will be plenty of children to make friends with.

"We're going to really enjoy it here," I tell Max.

He's looking up at the mountain that looms over the campsite with a worried look on his face.

"What's wrong?" I ask him.

"Shall we go up the mountain now to practice?"

"What do you mean practice?"

"My teacher Miss Rawlins says that if you want to get better at something, you have to practice it.

Like when we were learning the recorder in Music. If I don't practice mountain walking, I don't think I'll be very good at it tomorrow and you'll all be mad at me for being too slow."

"Don't be ridiculous," I tell him. "You're really starting to get on my nerves now." I stomp back to the tent and leave him there.

Later, when the tent is almost finished, I look over at Max and see that he's still standing exactly where I left him, staring up at the mountain.

Mum and Dad let us stay up late because we're all on holiday. We sit outside the tent and listen to an owl hooting somewhere in the night. Dad puts a lantern on that runs on gas. It makes a low hissing sound but it gives off a lot of light. That's all right for a while but then it attracts insects and Dad has to turn it off. There are moths scuttling all over the tent and trying to climb inside the lantern and there are little flies that bite and get in my hair.

"I think it's bedtime now, you two," Dad says finally. I'm really tired and I think Max is too because he's been quiet all night, not like his usual self at all. I suppose he needs more sleep than me because he's younger so if I'm tired, he must be exhausted.

We kiss Mum and Dad goodnight and climb into the tent. When I wriggle into my sleeping bag, I see that Max is still wide awake, staring up at the ceiling of the tent with wide eyes, his hands clasped together on his chest.

"What's wrong with you?" I ask him.

He doesn't turn to look at me or move any part of his body, other than his mouth, which makes him look like he's frozen. "Nothing. Go to sleep."

"Don't worry about tomorrow,' I tell him.

"I'm not worried."

"Yes you are, you said so earlier."

"Just go to sleep, Katy."

I let out a loud exasperated sigh to let him know I'm frustrated with him and snuggle deeper into my sleeping bag. Now that it's nighttime, it's gone a bit cold. I can hear Mum and Dad talking softly outside the tent. I can't hear what they're saying because I'm too tired to listen.

Before I fall asleep, I take a last look at Max. He's still wide awake. He'll regret it in the morning when he's too tired to walk up the mountain.

⚷

"Kate, wake up! Wake up!"

I open my eyes and look blearily up at Dad. He has a panicked look on his face that scares me instantly.

"It's your brother," he says. "He's missing."

I sit up and look over at Max's sleeping bag. He isn't there of course. Dad just told me he's missing but it's taking some time to sink in.

"Get dressed and meet us outside," Dad says. "We've got to look for him."

I hurriedly get dressed and climb out of the tent into the cold morning light. Mum is talking to some of the other campers, asking them if they've seen Max. She's got tears in her eyes.

"Come with me, Kate," Dad says. "We're going to check around the shop."

"I don't think he's there," I tell him. "I think he's gone up the mountain."

He looks at me quizzically. "What? Why ever would you say that?"

"He was talking about it yesterday. He said he wanted to practice mountain walking."

Dad looks at the mountain. It's so high that the top is hidden in mist and clouds. Dad's face looks even more worried than before. "Right, come on."

He marches off towards a wooden gate and I follow him.

The gate marks the beginning of the trail that leads up the mountain. Dad is almost running and I'm finding it hard to keep up. My breath feels hot in my chest and my legs ache, especially when the trail gets gradually steeper.

I don't know how long we've been walking when Dad finally stops and waits for me to catch up to him. I can't imagine that Max came this far on his own. We're really high up and at the side of the path, there's a steep drop that must be hundreds of feet down to a stream and lots of rocks.

"I think I was wrong, Dad," I say as I get to where he's standing. "There's no way Max came all the way up here."

He doesn't say anything and suddenly I think that maybe he didn't stop to let me catch up with him at all; he stopped because he saw something that made him stop.

"Dad?" I say, touching his shoulder.

He turns around and pulls me into a hug. "Don't look, Kate," he says and I feel his breath hitch and then feel his body shudder as he starts to cry. I cry as well even though I don't know what's wrong.

Then, even though I was told not to look, I move my face so I can see around Dad.

And I see the small, crumpled thing lying on the rocks below us.

It takes me almost a minute to realise it's my brother.

## CHAPTER 7

He isn't happy. The sun has been shining, melting the wintry landscape, and his headlights pick up water where last night there was snow and ice. He'd hoped to have his beautiful sleeping angel for at least another day but now that everything has thawed, he knows what he'll find when he gets to the depression in the moors. It won't be beautiful anymore.

When he arrives at the parking place by the moors, he gets out of the car and doesn't hesitate before setting off through the wet grass and heather. There is no cold wind blowing now that he can revel in, no harsh icy breath to freeze his skin. The world is wet and tepid.

The beauty he left in the depression will no longer be under ice, no longer beautiful.

When he reaches the depression, his worst fears are realised. The ice is gone and most of the water has been absorbed by the thawed ground, leaving the girl lying in a pool that barely covers her arms and legs.

Exposed to the air like this, she will soon spoil. The beauty that had been frozen in time by the ice will rot and decay. He has no interest in this.

Sighing, he turns away from the depression and makes his way back to the car. He feels hollow inside, lonely. He needs to create another work of beautiful art but he can't do that until the temperature plummets and the snow falls again.

Until then, he has to wait. Watch the weather forecast and wait.

He gets to the car, starts the engine, drives away without looking back. He'll never come to this exact spot again. Now that the ice is gone, it is a place of ugliness.

Besides, someone will find her soon, he has no doubt about that. Once his angels thaw, it doesn't take long before a hiker or a dog walker comes across them. He doesn't care; he was careful to leave no clues. And he has no interest in the girls after they thaw anyway.

Let the police have them so they can puzzle over questions like why someone would do such a thing.

No matter how much they try, they'll never understand.

They'll never catch him.

## CHAPTER 8

Detective Inspector Danica Summers—Dani to her friends and colleagues—steps over the fluttering police tape and walks towards the white tent that has been hastily set up to cover the body on the moors and preserve the scene as much as possible.

Apart from the tent and the tape, and the group of police officers milling about, it's beautiful up here; untamed wilderness overlooking Whitby in the distance and the grey, flat sea beyond that.

Dani spots DS Matt Flowers, by the tent and goes over to him. "Morning, Matt."

He gives her a nod. "Morning, Guv."

"What have we got?"

He pulls a small black notebook from his

pocket to make sure he doesn't miss anything while giving her the rundown. Matt lives closer to this area of the moors than Dani does so even though they both received the call from HQ at the same time, Matt got here first. If Dani knows Matt Flowers—and after two years of working together, she's sure she does—he's already questioned any witnesses present and gathered any relevant info from the SOCOs.

"Dog walker found her about an hour ago," he says, reading from the notes.

Dani checks her watch. 0530 hours. How early do people walk their bloody dogs around here?

"The dog led the owner straight to the body, which was lying in a pool of water in this depression," Matt continues, pointing out the dip in the land. "According to the SOCOs, she may have been there a while. The cold weather has slowed decomposition."

"Is it Amy Donovan?"

"I think so, Guv."

"Is there a ribbon?"

"Yes."

She closes her eyes and takes a deep breath of air to prevent her from spewing the expletive that's running around inside her head. She turns to the tent. "Right, let's have a look."

Matt pulls the tent flap back and Dani steps inside. The familiar sickly-sweet smell of death, mingled with the smell of dirt and water, hits her and she takes a moment to adjust. *Slow, shallow breaths through the nose*, she reminds herself.

Ray Rickman, head of the Scenes Of Crimes Officers, is standing just inside the tent entrance, dressed in white coveralls. When he sees Dani, he waves.

"Anything I need to know?" she asks him.

"Looks like your killer has struck again," he says. He gestures to the place on the ground which Dani has been steeling herself to look at. "See for yourself."

She turns towards the body, crouches down near the woman's head. "It's Amy Donovan," she says. She's seen plenty of photos of this young woman, photos of a happy, smiling young woman. But a person unknown somehow intersected with Amy's life and ended it abruptly. The woman in the water will never look into a camera again other than the ones used by the SOCOs and the Coroner.

Amy's hair floats in the water—the only part of

her that is still moving—and among the blonde tendrils floats a single red ribbon.

"Is there an injection site?" she asks Rickman. She already knows the answer; the Snow Killer sedates his victims before he drowns them.

Rickman nods. "There's a red mark at the base of her neck. Looks like he injected the sedative into her trapezius muscle. Probably diazepam, like the others."

Dani closes her eyes and let out a breath. Amy's name will now join the names of three other women on a whiteboard in the incident room at headquarters: Stephanie Wilmot, Nicola Patterson, and Angela Rayburn. All victims of the Snow Killer.

Dani has forbidden her team from using the monicker Red Ribbon Killer. She's witholding the facts surrounding the ribbons from the press. It's common knowledge that the first victim, Stephanie Wilmot, was found with a ribbon tied into her hair but not common knowledge that two other women—three now—have also been found with the exact same type of ribbon.

And even though there was a leak last year when some bright spark in the department told a journalist about the ribbons, Dani is determined to continue with her obfuscation of the facts, at least as far as the press is concerned. They still don't know about the sedative used on the women. That information hasn't been leaked. Probably isn't newsworthy enough for the sensationalist press anyway.

So her team has been ordered to refer to the killer of these women as the Snow Killer, not the Red Ribbon Killer, even in private.

"Cause of death appears to be drowning," Rickman says. "Whether in this water she's lying in or somewhere else, we won't know until we run some tests on what's in her lungs."

Drowning. Same COD as the other three women. There's no sign of sexual assault—at least there wasn't with the other three victims—and there are no signs of violence. He just takes them onto the moors and drowns them, always during a snowstorm. What is the bastard trying to achieve? What does the ribbon mean?

She stands up and turns to Rickman. "Get me those results as soon as you can, Ray."

"Of course," he says.

Dani pushes her way out of the tent and rejoins Matt. "Tell me about the dog walker."

He consults the notebook again. "Mr Andrew

Thomas, 62, from Little Beck. He brings his dog out onto the moors every morning and evening. He's in the back of the ambulance at the moment, being treated for shock. Do you want to talk to him?"

She shakes her head. "No, but get someone to check out his story. Does he always bring his dog here, to this spot, or does he vary his routine? If he comes here all the time, he might have seen something else on an earlier date, something he doesn't remember. We need to know if he saw anyone hanging around here, or any vehicles parked in the area."

"Yes, Guv." Matt makes a note and puts his notebook away. He gestures to the tent and says, "It's him, isn't it? The Snow Killer."

"Looks like it."

"What's our next move, Guv?"

"We need to go and tell Amy Donovan's next of kin that we've found a body. And we need to get a positive ID." She gestures to the police tape, where a number of journalists are already gathering with their cameras and microphones. "And we need to do it before these vultures start writing their own version of events."

She walks away from the tent, Matt in tow. She

isn't looking forward to telling Mr and Mrs Donovan that their daughter is dead. She can't imagine how it might feel to be told that a loved one's life has been snatched away by a killer.

As soon as she steps over the police tape, questions are thrown at her by the journalists and microphones are thrust into her face. She pushes them away and simply says, "No comment."

**CHAPTER 9**

It's almost lunchtime and I'm sitting in front of *Falcon House,* making notes on a legal pad and considering taking a break, when my computer goes off. "No, no!" I throw the pad onto the desk and toss the pen on top of it. Pulling the computer screen forward on my desk, I check behind it to see if the power cable has come out but it all looks fine back there. Then I realise the flat is more silent than usual. There's no hum from the fridge. The bloody power's gone off.

I flick the light switch on and off to make sure. Nothing.

That means I'm going to have to go downstairs and tell Rob. Of course, if the power is out in the entire building, then he'll know. But I can't take that chance; I need to get on with my work.

I go out into the hallway and try the lights there. They're dead.

Sighing, I go downstairs to the first floor and try the hallway lights there as well. Also dead.

I can hear noises drifting up the stairs from the ground floor; someone banging loudly on a door and Ivy's voice shouting, "Answer the door, you ignorant lout!"

I go down to see what's going on. Ivy is pounding on Rob's door with the heel of her hand. When she sees me, she jerks a thumb at the door. "He's not answering, dear. My electrics have gone off."

"So have mine," I tell her.

"Exactly the same thing happened the other day," she says. "I was sitting watching my stories and then all of sudden the telly goes off. And he —" she points at Rob's door, "tells me it's because of the wind and we just have to wait for it to come back on again."

"The other day? I don't remember the power going off."

"It was the evening before you moved in, dear. And let me tell you something: cats are supposed to be able to see in the dark but Winston was scared to death. He hid under the sofa for most of the evening. So I was sitting in the dark with a frightened cat and no telly until almost ten o' clock!"

"That sounds very inconvenient," I say, not sure that Rob North can be blamed for a power cut.

"I've a good mind to send a letter to his parents, tell them what a rubbish job he's doing. I'm sure they'd be interested to know about him leaving us without electricity." She raises her voice when she says this and directs her words at the door, as if Rob is behind it, listening.

"Maybe he's gone out," I suggest.

"I don't think so, dear. He only goes out at night, like a bloody vampire."

I walk past Ivy to the main door and check the parking area. My Mini is the only car out there.

"His car's not there," I tell Ivy.

She frowns. "Isn't it? I didn't hear it drive off."

"I heard it this morning, at about half past one."

"Oh yes, I heard that, dear."

"Maybe he didn't come back."

"He came back half an hour later." She taps her ear. "I told you, I could hear a pin drop. My memory might not be what it used to be but my hearing is spot on."

"Well he must have left this morning while you were in the shower or something, so you didn't hear him."

She shrugs. "It's possible, I suppose."

"I'm not sure he can do much about a power outage anyway," I say. "We're probably going to just have to wait."

Ivy seems unsatisfied by that. "Well I'd offer you a cup of tea, dear but the kettle won't work." She turns to shuffle back ot her flat.

"You could boil some water in a saucepan," I suggest. "The hob runs on gas." I can't bear to think of her sitting in her flat alone without even a cup of tea to keep her warm.

"Oh yes, so it does." She grins at me and waves me over to her flat. "Come on, I'll make us a nice cuppa."

I follow her inside, where Winston is rolling a plastic ball around the floor and pouncing on it.

She goes into the kitchen and puts a pan of water on the hob while I roll the ball for the cat and watch him chase it. When he catches it, he gives it a couple of jabs with his paw and then looks at me, waiting for me to roll it again.

I roll it under the sofa and he goes scurrying after it.

"I suppose you've seen the paper today," Ivy says from the kitchen. "Terrible business. Just terrible."

I haven't seen the news today, actually; I didn't roll out of bed until late and then I went straight to work on Falcon House. "No," I say to Ivy. "I haven't seen the paper. What's happened?"

She picks up a copy of The Mirror from the kitchen table and passes it to me. "There, you can see for yourself."

The headline on the front page, AMY DONOVAN LATEST VICTIM OF RED RIBBON KILLER, sits above a photo of a forensic tent on the moors. So they've found Amy at last and they were right about her not being alive.

"I suppose we'll have the police around here asking questions," Ivy says as she loads the teapot with teabags. "The last time they were here, I told them I'm an old lady who never gets out. How am I supposed to know anything about missing women? But they kept asking their questions anyway. Very confusing, they were."

"The police came here? To this house?"

"Yes, to ask about the missing woman."

"Amy Donovan?"

"No, not her. This was a couple of years ago, when that other one went missing." She frowns as if trying to remember something, then shakes her head. "No, I can't remember her name." She resumes her task of making the tea.

I wonder why the police came to this house in particular. Were they following a lead or just carrying out door-to-door inquiries?

"They wanted to know everything," Ivy continues. "One of them asked for my name, date of birth, all that kind of thing. I said, 'Never mind my date of birth, you cheeky young man,' but he was quite insistent."

"Did they question everyone in the building?"

She ponders this for a moment, then nods. "I suppose so. Well, all except him. Rob. He was out at the time. They said they'd come back later."

I take my phone out of my pocket with the intention of looking up when the first woman went missing but the Wi-Fi from my flat doesn't reach down here and there's no data signal out here in the middle of nowhere.

Even if I was in my own flat, there wouldn't be any Wi-Fi, I remind myself; the power's off so the hub won't be working. For the first time, I feel isolated in this house on the moors.

Ivy lays out the cups and saucers on the table and I bring the pot.

She sits down and I pour the tea as she continues. "I told them, 'If there's anyone around here who's dodgy, it's him. Rob, the landlord.' But they didn't seem all that interested in what I was telling them."

"Did they come back to question him later?" I ask.

She shrugs. "I don't know."

"Surely you don't think he could be involved in anything like that," I say. "I mean, he's a bit creepy and everything but—"

"I wouldn't trust him as far as I can throw him. I once saw him hurl a snowball at Winston. At a poor defenceless cat! I ask you, what kind of person does that?" She takes a sip of tea and adds, "I even offered to let the police into his flat so they could have a look around but they weren't interested in the slightest. Some detectives they were!"

"They're not allowed to search just anyone's flat. They need a warrant. How were you going to let them in? Have you got a key?"

She winks at me and taps the side of her nose conspiratorially. "Well, I'm not supposed to have one."

I lean forward and lower my voice. "But have you?"

She nods slowly. "Fred and Wanda used to live in this flat, you see. Before they moved to Spain. When I moved in, what did I find lurking at the back of one of the kitchen drawers? A set of keys. They either left them here for Rob and he didn't know about them or they just put them in the drawer and forgot about them."

"And you still have them?"

"Of course. They're still in the same drawer, behind my knives and forks. I thought I'd hold onto them in case I ever needed them."

"And have you? Used them, I mean."

Ivy shakes her head. "No, never had the need to."

I'm still wondering why the police came here and questioned everyone. Northmoor House is remote. For the police to come here specifically, they must have had a good reason. I remember them combing the moors behind the house. "Ivy, was one of the dead women found near here? Is that why the police came asking questions?"

She looks up from her teacup. "Hmm? No, dear, when they came here, they hadn't found anyone. She was still missing."

I make a mental note to check the date once the Wi-Fi comes back on. The fact that the police came here asking questions might not mean anything at all but the part of my mind that needs answers has been engaged now and I can't ignore it.

Outside, a car pulls onto the gravel, its engine rumbling.

"That's him," Ivy says. "I'd know the sound of that noisy old thing anywhere" She gets up from the table. "I'm going to give him a piece of my mind. What does he think he's doing swanning off while we're sitting here with no electricity?"

I follow her to the door. Winston peeks out at us from under the sofa, where he's been playing with his ball.

Ivy puts her hand on the door handle but doesn't open the door yet. She waits until Rob's footsteps in the hallway reach the door and then she flings it open and shouts at him, "I want a word with you!"

Startled, he whirls around to face her, dropping the cardboard box he's carrying. It crashes to the floor. "You stupid old bat!" He crouches down and picks it up. It's open and I can see a tangle of cables and wires inside. There's also an old keyboard in there and what looks like a webcam.

"Never mind calling me names," Ivy says, "How about fixing the electrics? We've been sitting in the cold and the dark for ages."

He straightens up and pulls the baseball cap down over his head with one hand, the box under his other arm. "I told you before, I can't control the national grid. Ring up the electric company and report it. Don't come to me with problems I can't fix."

"Can't fix or won't fix?"

"I think he's right, Ivy," I say, putting a gentle hand on her shoulder. "We're just going to have to wait for it to come back on."

"See," Rob says, gesturing to me with his free hand. "Listen to Katy."

"It's Kate," I tell him firmly.

"Whatever." He digs his keys out of the back pocket of his jeans and opens the door to his flat.

"Don't you walk away from me," Ivy calls after him.

Rob steps through the doorway, turns to face

us, and gives us a salute. "*Hasta la vista*." He closes the door.

"What the bloody hell is that supposed to mean?" Ivy asks.

"I think it means we won't be seeing him again any time soon and he isn't interested in the fact that the power is off."

"Useless!" she says, turning around and shuffling back into the flat. "I don't know why I expected anything different from the likes of him. He's always been the same. I think that accident sent him a bit funny in the head."

We go back to Ivy's kitchen and finish our tea. When we're done, I wash the cups in the sink and put them on the draining board to dry. Ivy sits on the sofa and stares at the dead TV as if willing it to come back to life.

"I've got an idea," I say while I'm drying my hands. "Why don't we go for a drive into town?"

She looks at me with a worried expression on her face. "Town?"

"Yes, we can find a nice warm cafe. It beats sitting here in the cold."

She mulls it over for a minute or two. "Well, I suppose so." She doesn't seem very certain and that makes me wonder just how long it is since she last went out.

"I'll go up and get my coat and gloves," I tell her. "See you back here in five minutes?"

Ivy nods slowly. "All right. But what about Winston?"

"I'm sure he'll be fine for an hour or two."

She nods again. "All right."

I go upstairs and grab my coat, hat, and gloves. Without any heating on in the flat, the temperature is dropping. I hadn't planned to spend the afternoon in town with my neighbour but then I hadn't planned on a power cut making it impossible for me to work either. And I can't leave her alone in a cold flat staring at a blank TV screen.

When I go back down to her flat, I find Ivy waiting for me just inside her door. She's got a thick coat and a knitted green hat with matching gloves and scarf on.

"You look prepared," I say.

"You have to be at my age, dear."

We go out to the Mini and set off along the road that leads into town. The road seems busier than usual and I guess it's because of the discovery of Amy Donovan. There are probably journalists and news crews here from all over the country. This is the kind of story I would have covered during my days at the Manchester Recorder. I suppose I miss some of the excitement from those days. The Amy Donovan case would have had me hightailing it over to Whitby to piece together whatever scraps of information I could find into a story.

Now I sit at a desk all day and advise other writers about *their* stories. Not exactly thrilling.

What is thrilling, though, is seeing Ivy's face as we drive along the road. She has a contented smile that tells me just how happy she is to be doing something other than sitting in her flat watching TV.

"Shall I put the radio on?" I ask her.

"Yes, that would be nice."

I hit the button and the news comes on. A female voice is talking. It sounds like she's reading from a prepared statement. "*In the early hours of this morning, a body was found on the moors. After a positive identification by family members, we can confirm that this was the body of Amy Donovan, who disappeared from her home four days ago. Detectives are working around the clock to apprehend the person or persons responsible for Miss Donovan's death, so that her family might have some closure. If anyone has any information about the whereabouts of Amy during the last four days, or has any other information that might be useful to solving this crime, please contact the North Yorkshire Police incident room.*"

She reads out a phone number.

The newsreader says, "*That was Chief Constable Lisa Waring of North Yorkshire Police appealing for help in the Amy Donovan murder inquiry.*"

"Look." Ivy says, pointing to the moors on our right. "That must be where they found her."

I glance out of my window and see, in the distance, a white tent surrounded by dark figures. Parked on a road nearby are a number of police vehicles.

We've only been driving for about five minutes. That's how close Amy Donovan's body was to Northmoor House all this time. Just a five minute drive away. Whoever put her there was also that close to the house.

"If I knew who it was, I wouldn't call the police," Ivy says.

I look at her, not sure what she means by that. "Why not?"

"He wouldn't last that long once I got my hands on him."

# CHAPTER 10

"Get a shot of the abbey, Pete," Jillian Street says to her cameraman. They're walking along Pier Road, getting a few snaps of Whitby after spending the morning on the moors trying to get someone from the police to talk about the body that's been discovered up there.

Jillian's instincts tell her it's Amy Donovan but nobody in authority is saying anything.

She's been in Whitby for two days now, following the story of Amy Donovan. If Amy turns out to be the latest victim of the Red Ribbon Killer, then that's all the better. Serial killer stories sell better than "girl freezes to death on moors" stories and Jillian is hoping to grab a scoop that she can sell to the highest bidder.

Her freelance journalism has had its up and downs but certainly more of the latter than the former. After leaving the Daily Star five years ago, she spent most of her time trying to track down the Eastbourne Ripper, following the trail of bloodshed and shattered lives he left in his wake.

But after the Ripper, aka Leonard Sims, was caught and incarcerated, there's been a scarcity of stories juicy enough to interest the big tabloids. Only the Red Ribbon Killer has piqued the public's interests and he only kills in winter, the inconsiderate bastard.

Still, Jillian has shifted her focus from the Eastbourne Ripper to the Red Ribbon Killer and is considering writing a book. So the shots Pete is currently getting of Whitby may end up in her magnum opus someday establishing the setting of Red's dastardly deeds.

Pete is no David Bailey when it comes to photography, or videography for that matter, but he's handy to have around. Jillian would find it difficult to shove a microphone into someone's face and have to worry about the video and audio at the same time.

So she hires Pete—a wedding photographer in his hometown of Birmingham when not working for Jillian—to do all of that stuff while she concentrates on the thing she excels at: writing an attention-grabbing headline and a gut-punching story.

So far, she hasn't come up with anything newsworthy from today's early-morning excursion to the moors. Detective Inspector Summers wasn't saying anything, as usual, and neither were her team. The only headline Jillian scribbled in her notebook was *Police Baffled By Girl On Moors* but that's already a non-starter; the police have just announced that they know the person they found this morning is Amy Donovan.

So it's back to square one: try to get interviews with Amy's family, attempt to get some juicy morsel from the police, and hope that some nugget of information—something that no one else knows regarding the case—will come her way. It's a long shot but she lives in hope.

"Anything else, Jillian?" Pete asks, lowering his camera and looking at her with a pained expression on his face. "I'm starving."

She sighs in frustration. It's like working with a five-year-old child. "All right, Pete, go and get yourself some fish and chips or something. I'll meet you back at the car park in an hour."

His face breaks into a grin and he virtually runs to the nearest chippy.

Jillian wanders along the road towards the pier, mulling over the title of her future book. *She Wore a Red Ribbon*? No, too obscure. *The Girls on the Moors*? Too Gothic. *A Ribbon Red*? Too literary.

She casts a glance at the shops in front of her and does a double take when she sees someone from her past, someone she hasn't seen in a long time.

"Kate Lumley!"

Kate is gazing into the window of an antiques shop and looks up when she hears her name. She sees Jillian and recognition dawns on her face. "Jillian, what are you doing here?"

"I could ask you the same question," Jillian says, drawing Kate into a brief hug. Part of her wonders if Kate is here for the same reason she is, to work the Red Ribbon Killer story. Another part of her thinks that unlikely; Kate's credentials in the world of journalism have been reduced to cinders since she published that dreadful story about Simon Coates.

Maybe Kate is in Whitby because she's hiding from the press. There are sure to be reporters trying to get her reaction to the arrest of Stella

Coates. Well if she's here trying to escape the papers, she's in the wrong place. The Red Ribbon Killer has brought every journalist and wannabe from all over the country to the little seaside town.

"I live here now," Kate says, blowing Jillan's theory out of the water.

"Oh, how lovely," she says, trying to hide her disappointment that Kate isn't on the run after all. She might have been able to get an exclusive interview out of it. "A bit of a change from Manchester."

Kate nods. "And I'm working for a publisher now."

"Nice. Listen, do you want to grab a drink? My photographer is gorging his face on fish and chips at the moment so I'm free for an hour or so."

"Sounds good but unfortunately, I can't. I'm just waiting for my friend. She's getting some fish for her cat."

"Oh, maybe another time then." She was going to try to get a few drinks into Kate and broach the subject of Stella Coates, ask a few innocent questions that sound like friendly concern. It probably wouldn't have worked anyway; Kate will see past any thinly-veiled attempt to get information from her. She's worked the crime beat far too long to be taken in by such tactics.

And the friendly concern thing wouldn't work either. They've crossed paths a few times during their careers but they're hardly busom buddies.

"Well you've got my number," Jillian says airily. "Call me if you fancy catching up sometime."

"Will do," Kate says, offering her a friendly smile. Jillian tries to decipher its true meaning but can't. Maybe Kate is just being friendly. Not everyone is disingenuous.

She turns away from her old acquaintance and looks for Pete. He's leaning against the iron railing that borders the harbour, watching the boats as he eats his fish and chips from a cardboard box.

"Give me one of those," Jillian says, taking a chip from the box and popping it into her mouth. She regrets it almost immediately. The chip is so hot she has to open her mouth so the cold air can cool it on her tongue.

"Hey, get your own." He turns away, using his substantial body to block her from his food.

"Calm down, Pete, it's only a chip for God's sake."

She taps him on the shoulder so he'll turn to

face her. He doesn't and continues eating with his back towards her.

"Pete, look who I've just seen."

He turns his head to look at her over his shoulder.

"Over there," Jillian says. "Outside the antiques shop."

He looks across the street and frowns. "Who's that?"

"That is Kate Lumley. She used to be a reporter until she falsely accused someone of murdering his own son."

"Oh, her."

"Yes, her. Now get a couple of shots of her for me."

He looks at the camera hanging from his neck and at the box of chips in his hands.

"I'll hold those for you," she offers.

He looks at her suspiciously. "You can hold them but don't have any, okay?"

"Fine. I'm on a diet anyway."

Handing her the chips, he takes the lens cap off his Canon and starts snapping pictures of Kate.

"What's she doing here?" he asks, adjusting his zoom lens. "I thought she got kicked off that paper she was working for."

"She told me she's just living here but I can't believe she's in the middle of serial killer territory and not investigating what's going on. That's not the Kate Lumley I know."

"Maybe she's changed." He finishes taking the photos and puts the lens cap back on his camera.

"Nobody changes that much," she says, taking another chip from the box and popping it into her mouth.

**CHAPTER 11**

When Ivy and I get back to Northmoor House at half past four, the roads are pitch black and I can see a few flakes of snow fluttering in the headlight beams. We spent most of the afternoon in a coffee shop and then visited the fishmongers where Ivy got a fresh piece of cod for her cat. She seems exhausted by the excursion and she's looking forward to getting back to Winston but I think she enjoyed herself.

The most welcome sight when I pull into the parking area is the lit windows in Northmoor House. "The power's back on," I tell Ivy.

She gives me a weary smile.

I help her inside and say goodbye to her at her door. As she goes into her flat, I hear her say,

"Winston, I've got a treat for you." Then the cat lets out a long meow, either in appreciation of the fresh fish or in anger at being left alone for a while.

I go up to my flat and take off my jacket and hat, throwing them onto the sofa before sitting at my desk and switching the computer on. I might as well get back a couple of the hours I lost when the power died.

As I skim over the sections of *The Secrets of Falcon House* I was reading before I was interrupted, I reach for my legal pad and pen. My hand falls on the pad but the pen isn't there. I look over at the pad. The pen is gone.

Frowning, I push my chair back and check the floor under the desk. It isn't there either.

"It can't just disappear," I tell myself, scanning the floor all around the desk. "It has to be here somewhere." But there's no pen to be seen.

The pen itself is nothing special—just a black ballpoint from a pack of twelve I got at the supermarket—but I need to know if it's here or not.

Because if not, someone has taken it.

*Don't jump to conclusions. Maybe you took it into the kitchen when you made a drink and left it there.*

But when I check, the pen isn't in there either. Nor is it in the bathroom or living room.

*Has someone been in here?*

I inspect each room, looking for signs that anything has been disturbed. But unlike Annie Wilkes in *Misery*, I don't have an ornamental ceramic penguin that always faces due south. If someone came in here and moved stuff around, I probably wouldn't know about it just from the position of the knick-knacks in the flat.

I do a quick inventory of our possessions, trying to remember exactly how the flat looked when I left it earlier. Nothing else seems to be missing. Just the pen.

I tell myself I'm overreacting; who'd break into the flat just to take a cheap pen? It doesn't make sense. The pen has to be somewhere in here; I just can't find it. But a second search on and around the desk reveals nothing. The pen has vanished.

I go to the front door and check the lock. It's intact and there are no marks on the doorframe indicating forced entry.

*You knew there wouldn't be. The person you suspect has a key. And he probably saw you leave with Ivy. He had ample time to let himself in and wander around.*

*But why take the pen?*

The answer hits me in an instant. *As a trophy.*

Rob must have let himself into the flat and, while he was here, decided to take something personal to me. The pen itself has no value—it's just a cheap ballpoint out of a supermarket packet —but the fact that I was using it makes it a personal item.

*He wants something that I've touched. That I've been handling.*

The thought sickens me. I don't know what to do. I want to go down to his flat and face him, demand that he gives me my pen back and then maybe call the police. He can't just let himself into my home. It's trespassing.

But he'll simply deny it. Even if the pen is in his flat, I couldn't prove it's mine; there must be a million pens identical to that one. Is that why he took that particular object?

If he'd taken one of the personal items we own —like one of the framed photographs of Greg and me or the porcelain dolphin I bought during a holiday in Greece—it could be traced back to me if discovered.

The pen, however, can't. No one could prove that's my pen, unless they fingerprinted it and checked for my prints, and what police force would fingerprint a cheap old ballpoint pen? Even the presence of my prints wouldn't mean anything; Rob could say it's the pen I signed the lease with so of course my prints are on it.

So there's no point going down there and having it out with Rob. He might even get pleasure out of my frustration. I won't give him the satisfaction.

I close the flat door and wonder what I *can* do if I don't confront him directly. I'm an investigative journalist, after all, so I'll do what I do best: investigate. Ivy seems to think Rob is "dodgy" and considering my missing pen, I have to agree. He's been in the flat while I wasn't here. If he'd slipped in and out without touching anything, I'd have been none the wiser but he made a mistake by taking a trophy. Now I'm onto him. What else has he been up to?

I take my seat at the desk and begin typing into the search engine. Maybe I can get a bit of background information on Rob North. After an hour of digging, I haven't come up with much beyond an old photo that someone in Rob's class at school has posted on Facebook. A number of students are sitting on a row of desks posing and in the background, Rob is walking by and looking at the camera as if surprised to find himself part of the photo. He looks about twelve years old but he already has the large scar on his head, so the accident Ivy referred to must have happened when he was no more than a child.

Whereas most of the people in the picture have been tagged, Rob's name is simply listed, suggesting he doesn't have a Facebook account. It's going to be difficult to track his digital footprint if he doesn't use social media or uses a pseudonym.

I decide to change tack and type in Fred and Wanda's names, along with the qualifier "Spain." I get some hits. It seems Rob's parents aren't quite as camera shy as their son. They at least have a Facebook page. It only shows me a few pictures because I'm not on their friends list but the few I can see show a couple in their late fifties sitting by a pool in the sun.

Fred has scars on his arms and shoulders, starkly contrasted against his tanned skin. Wanda is wearing a long-sleeved kaftan and a wide-brimmed hat and I wonder if she has similar scarring to her husband and son.

Scars aside, the Internet doesn't give me any more information on Rob North or his parents. I imagine he would have had a tough childhood. Children can be cruel when someone stands out in some way and I guess that the scar across his head would have made Rob an easy target for schoolyard bullies.

Is that why he uses a pseudonym on the Net? I can't imagine that he has no online presence.

Deciding that an Internet search isn't going to give me any easy answers, I turn my attention to the Red Ribbon Killer. Why had the police been around here asking questions when the first woman went missing? I can understand them making house to house inquiries in town but Northmoor House is virtually in the middle of nowhere. They would have had to make a special journey to come here. Why did they think it worth their time to do so?

I type in Red Ribbon Killer and also Snow Killer, since the killer is known by both names. A wealth of information appears on the screen, so much I barely know where to start.

To narrow the results, I add the search term "first victim." A photograph of a young blonde woman appears on the right of the screen. She's smiling at the camera in what appears to be a professional photography studio. Her hair looks like she just came from a salon and her makeup is immaculate. This picture was taken for a special occasion, at a happy time during this young woman's life. Now it bears the legend: *Stephanie Wilmot, first victim of the Snow Killer.*

I click a couple of links and piece together Stephanie's story.

According to the news and police reports, Stephanie Wilmot was driving from York, where she'd been visiting a friend, to her home in Westerdale, a village on the moors. She never arrived. Her husband, who'd been waiting expectantly for Stephanie's return, had finally called the police. A snowstorm had descended upon the moors, so he was worried that his wife had become stuck somewhere between York and Westerdale.

The police found Stephanie's car five miles from her house. It had skidded into a ditch by the side of the road. Stephanie wasn't inside. Fearing she'd wandered off into the storm, the police began a frantic search of the area but, because of the weather, had to call it off after a couple of hours. There were no tracks around Stephanie's car to indicate which way she'd gone because fresh snowfall had obscured everything.

Her body was found four days later—on Christmas Eve—floating in a half-frozen pond twenty miles away from where her car had been found. Stephanie had drowned in the pond. The police might have concluded that she'd wandered onto the ice and fallen through except for the fact that a red ribbon had been tied into her hair. According to her husband, Stephanie owned no such ribbon nor had she been wearing one when she left her friend's house. This small detail was enough for the officer in charge of the case— Detective Inspector Danica Summers—to open a murder investigation.

I bring up a map of Whitby and the surrounding area. I find Westerdale in the middle of the moors. It's miles away from Whitby and Northmoor House. So why would the police come here asking questions?

Hitting the images button, I find more pictures of Stephanie Wilmot, as well as pictures of two women who fell victim to the Snow Killer in the winter of 2018, Nicola Patterson and Angela Rayburn. There's a definite look shared by the three ladies; long blonde hair, blue eyes, high cheekbones. No wonder Nia told me to be careful; I fit the killer's "type" exactly.

I also find photos of the areas of the moors where the bodies were found and a picture taken this morning of the scene where Amy Donovan was found. This photograph, taken by a journalist, shows the white tent Ivy and I saw when we drove into town. A number of police officers are standing around the tent and guarding the crime scene tape. The journalist has focused on a fair-haired woman in a long coat and dark blue scarf. She's walking away from the tent with her hands in her pockets, coming towards the crime scene tape. I click on the photo and am taken to the article it's part of, an article in the Whitby Gazette. Beneath the photo are the words *DI Danica Summers, head of the investigation into the Snow Killer murders.*

Had this woman been to Northmoor House asking questions two years ago?

I'm still pondering this when I hear a key in the front door. I swivel around in my chair, wondering for a moment if Rob North is going to walk through the door.

It swings open and Greg steps into the flat. He sees me at the desk and waves. "Hard at work?"

I close the websites. After what happened with Simon Coates, I don't want Greg thinking I'm sticking my nose into things that don't concern me. "I'm done. How was work?"

"Great. Fancy going out for dinner?"

"Okay," I say, "What's the occasion?"

"My boss told me today that he likes to get to know all his new members of staff and their families so he's invited us to go out for dinner with him and his wife Marcia."

"Sounds good. So are we going to a restaurant in Middlesbrough?"

Greg shakes his head. "They're coming here. To Whitby. Terry says he knows the owner of a seafood restaurant in town. The Captain's Table. We're going to meet them there at eight."

I check the time on my phone. It's almost half past six. Barely time to have a bath and get ready.

Greg goes into the kitchen and I hear him curse.

"What's wrong?"

"The bloody ceiling's leaking again! I thought Rob had fixed it."

I go in there and see drips coming from the same place on the ceiling, dropping into the sink at a slow but steady rhythm.

"I don't understand. It's hardly even snowing. There's just a few flakes in the air." Greg says.

"There must be a burst pipe up there or something." He sighs. "I'll go down and tell Rob."

"We can mention it to Rob on our way out," I suggest. At least if Rob sorts it while we're at dinner with Greg's boss, I won't have to listen to him stomping around over our ceiling.

"Fine," Greg says. "But he'd better fix it properly this time or I'm going to complain to the owners."

I head to the bathroom. As I open the door, Greg says, "They live in Spain don't they?"

"Yes, that's right," I say, remembering the pictures of the scarred couple by the pool.

"That's the trouble," Greg says. "They're so far away, this place is out of sight, out of mind. Rob probably thinks he can do what he wants and his parents will never find out. Well, he forgets that their address is on the lease. I'll be writing them a strongly-worded letter if this leak isn't fixed."

I smile. Greg's fighting spirit is present and correct.

I run a hot bath, scented with peach and mango bubbles, and climb in. As I lie there looking up at the ceiling, I'm glad we decided to wait before telling Rob about the leak. It might sound crazy but I wouldn't be able to lie here naked while he walks over the ceiling just above my head. I'd feel like his eyes were able to see me through the attic floor.

No matter how crazy that thought is, I sink lower in the tub and manoeuvre the bubbles so they completely cover my body.

## CHAPTER 12

Dani gets home at half past six. As she parks the Land Rover on the drive outside her cottage, she's glad the snow is light tonight. Heavy snow seems to trigger the killer for some reason and the last thing she needs right now is another missing woman. She'd like Amy Donovan to be the last victim this killer gets. She wants to catch him before he strikes again. But she needs time to do that and at the moment she has no leads. It's like the bastard just appears and disappears with the snow.

Maybe the video chat she's scheduled with Maya Cho in fifteen minutes will shine some light on the situation. Maya, a leading criminal psychologist who sometimes consults with the force, was sent the files on the Snow Killer's four victims this morning after agreeing to look at the case.

Dani gets out of the Land Rover and tries the front door of the cottage. It's unlocked. Scowling, she pushes the door open and steps inside. "Charlie, I told you to keep this bloody door locked."

Charlotte, her nineteen-year-old daughter, is sitting at the kitchen table with her head in a textbook and a pen in her mouth. She looks up and smiles sheepishly. "Sorry, Mum."

Dani locks the door behind her and as she does so, hears the skitter of claws on the kitchen floor. She turns to face Barney and Jack, her two german shepherds, as they bound towards her. They crouch before her, tails wagging furiously, waiting to be petted. Dani strokes their heads and rubs behind their ears. She supposes the dogs would protect Charlotte if an intruder entered the cottage. They're fiercely loyal to Dani and, by extension, her daughter.

"Are you studying?" Dani asks, going into the kitchen.

"Yeah, I don't want to fall behind," Charlotte says.

She's not going to tell her daughter to stop studying while she's here on Christmas break but Dani thinks Charlotte is worrying too much. Her Chemistry degree is going just fine and she'll probably be graduating with honors.

"How long have you been hitting the books?" she asks.

Charlotte checks the clock on the wall. "Most of the afternoon, I guess."

"How about we go out for dinner tonight?"

Charlotte looks suspicious. "We never go out."

"I know but you'll be going back to Birmingham soon and I'll miss you. Let's have some mother-daughter time."

Charlotte shrugs. "Okay, where are we going?"

Dani wracks her brain. There aren't many restaurants open in the evening in Whitby this early in the year. "How about the Captain's Table?"

"Okay." Charlotte closes her textbook.

"I just need to do something first; a Skype call with a psychologist. I shouldn't be too long. Then we'll go."

"I'll get ready."

"Let the dogs out first."

Charlotte opens the back door. Barney and Jack run outside. The automatic security light goes on as the dogs run beneath it, lighting up the spacious back garden. The garden is larger than the cottage itself. After her husband's death three years ago, Dani decided she had to downsize after realising she was unable to live any longer in the large house they'd lived in as a family. There were too many memories packed within those walls.

She waited until Charlotte went to university in Birmingham, because she didn't want the poor girl to have any more stress after losing a parent to cancer. Once Charlotte was settled away from home, Dani bought the cottage. It was small but had enough room for her and the dogs and Charlotte when she was home from uni.

The one thing Dani refused to downsize was her garden. The dogs need space to exercise and play. They're big animals and, as such, need a big garden.

And Dani loves gardening. In the spring and summer months, she spends hours pottering about outside. She grows flowers in the borders and tends the large apple tree at the bottom of the garden. It's her escape from the harsh realities she faces on the job and in her personal life.

"I'll take this call in my bedroom," she tells Charlotte. "Don't take all the hot water."

She goes into the room and closes the door. Her bedroom is small, like the rest of the cottage, but enough for her needs. Her bed is a double, the same one she shared with Shaun when he was alive, the one she knows beyond a shadow of a doubt she will never share with anyone else.

Her laptop is on the bedside table. Dani opens it and places it on the bed, sitting cross-legged before it as she open up the Skype app and waits for Maya Cho's call. Five minutes later, it comes and Dani answers it.

The woman who appears on the screen is in her forties with a black bob hairstyle and blue-rimmed glasses. She has an air of confidence, but not arrogance, that is common to people at the top of their profession. "Good evening, detective."

"Please, call me Dani."

Maya nods. "And I'm Maya."

"Did you look at the case files?"

"Yes, I went through them first thing this morning."

"And what can you tell me?"

"I can tell you that these four murders were almost certainly carried out by the same perpetrator. He's trying to create something, or should I say *re*create something every time he takes a victim. It's something from his past. I would say it's something that occurred while he was a child, or in a crucial stage of his emotional development. And it's something very visual. When he puts the red ribbon into the victim's hair and places her into a body of water, he's recreating a visual tableau."

"So this is something he's seen in the past?"

"Yes, it's something that affected him deeply. He connects strong emotions to this image of a woman wearing a red ribbon floating in water. Sexual emotions, most likely."

"But there's no sign of sexual assault or molestation," Dani says.

"No, there doesn't have to be. The person who did this—" she holds up one of the crimes scene photos of Angela Rayburn floating in an icy pond, red ribbon frozen to her hair, "has a paraphilic disorder."

"Paraphilic disorder?" Dani asks, grabbing a notebook and writing it down. "I'm sorry, Maya, could you explain that to me in layman's terms?"

"Of course. A paraphilia is when someone has an abnormal sexual desire. It usually emerges during adolescence, when a person's sex drive is beginning to develop. The drive can sometimes become attached to something inappropriate. Have you heard of toonophilia?"

"No," Dani admits.

"It's a slang term for when a person is sexually attracted to a cartoon character they might have seen on TV while they were developing emotionally and sexually. The attraction carries on into adulthood. Instead of a cartoon character, the perpetrator in this case saw an image that resembles this—" she holds up the photo of Angela Rayburn again, "and attached emotions to it."

"So he was young at the time?"

"I'd say he was between twelve and seventeen years of age when this emotional attachment was formed."

"But we're looking for an adult," Dani says. "Why has he waited so long to go from seeing whatever he saw that caused the—" she consults her notebook, "paraphilia to acting out on it?"

"It may have lain dormant inside him until something happened to cause it to surface."

"A trigger," Dani says.

Maya nods. "The paraphilia may have manifested in subtle ways throughout the perpetrator's life—sexual fantasies for example—

but once the trigger occurred, his emotions would have forced him to act. The fantasies wouldn't be enough anymore; he'd have to try to recreate his desire in real life if he was to continue deriving pleasure from it."

"So this trigger," Dani says, "is something that awakened his desire."

"Inflamed it would be a more accurate description. The desire would always have been there, just at a lower level, something that he could deal with. And the trigger was probably something simple, like seeing a blonde-haired woman wearing a red ribbon. He could have seen that same woman every day with no effect upon his psyche until the day he sees her wearing a red ribbon in her hair. Then he's triggered. And the result is in the case files you sent me this morning."

Dani makes more notes, feeling she has a better understanding of what she's dealing with. She'd already guessed that the killer was constantly trying to create a particular scene and that some sort of trigger had set him off—she's seen enough *Wire In The Blood* and *Criminal Minds* to understand how these things work—but to have her theories confirmed by Maya lets her know for certain that she's on the right track.

"What about the snow?" she asks. "He always strikes during a snowstorm. Is the weather a trigger as well?"

"Many killers have an environmental trigger such as the weather or phase of the moon," Maya says. "This man has been dubbed the Snow Killer for a reason. He seems to only strike in winter and only during a heavy snowfall. The snow itself isn't necessarily a trigger, although it might be, but is probably an element he needs to complete the visual scene he's trying to recreate. So the first time he saw a woman in the water with a red ribbon, it was probably snowing heavily. Now, he needs that to be a part of the tableau, to make the scene he creates match his memory of the initial encounter."

Dani scribbles more notes on the pad. "Could he evolve and carryout the killings without the snow?"

"That's very unlikely. He has a script he needs to follow. If he carried out a killing in the summer, for example, it wouldn't feel satisfying to him because it wouldn't be close to what he remembers of the initial encounter, the encounter to which he attaches so much emotion."

Dani nods, glad that at least the bastard is restricted by certain weather patterns. If he was able to kill all year round, there'd probably be a lot more murdered women. "What else can you tell me about him, Maya?"

"What do you want to know?"

"His name and address."

Maya smiles. "I've put together a brief profile but I'll need more time to make it more complete."

"Anything you have could be invaluable."

The profiler consults a notebook offscreen and says, "He's probably a loner. He has trouble maintaining long-term relationships, especially emotional ones, because of the paraphilia. If he had girlfriends in the past, the relationships would have been short-lived. He may have displayed deviant sexual tendencies, probably involving suffocation, strangulation, or drowning."

"Would he have a record?" Dani asks. She knows that killers sometimes evolve from minor offences to the act of killing. "If I search through old cases of flashing or rape, am I going to find him somewhere in those files?"

"That's unlikely. He's fixated on a very

particular thing and flashing or rape wouldn't come close to what he wants. You'd be better served to look at complaints to the police by women who say their boyfriend or partner has tried to strangle or drown them. The partner might have tried to laugh it off as some form of sexual exploration that went too far when questioned but it could be that he was rehearsing his eventual crimes."

Dani notes that down. Some members of her team aren't going to be very happy tomorrow when she asks them to trawl through old complaints going back years.

"If he has a job, it's probably something he can do alone," Maya says. "You're not going to find him working as part of a team or in a job that requires a lot of social interaction. He probably drives a vehicle that is utilitarian rather than flashy or expensive. It may be an SUV or something that has a four wheel drive capability, since he often visits remote places during bad weather. He also uses this vehicle to abduct his victims during a heavy snowfall so it has to be able to fulfil that purpose."

Dani writes the information on her notepad.

"As far as age goes, I'd guess that he's in his twenties or thirties, no older than that. If not athletic, he's at least very strong. All of his victims were sedated. Assuming he sedates them to control them when he first takes them, he may have to carry them to the body of water in which he drowns them." She looks up from her notes. "Regarding the sedation, it shows that for him, the act of killing isn't the aim here. It's merely a means to an end."

"What do you mean by that?" Dani asks.

"He isn't doing this for the thrill of the kill. Many serial killers enjoy the act of watching their victims' lives ebb away. In this case, the act of killing is just something he has to do to get the result he wants. That's probably why he sedates them: so they'll die without a struggle. He doesn't need to see fear in their eyes as they die or anything like that. He enjoys the fact that they're drowned rather than the fact that *he* drowned them. Does that make sense?"

Dani nods.

"That's all I have for now but I'll look at the case files again and call you if I have anything else to add."

"Thanks," Dani says, "This is really helpful."

"I hope you catch him," Maya says. She ends the video call and disappears from the screen.

Dani rereads her notes, crossing out and rewriting words that had been too hastily scribbled to be legible, and closes the laptop. She puts the notebook on the bedside table and sits back on the bed, waiting for Charlotte to finish in the bathroom so she can go in there and have a shower.

Today has not been a good one and she needs to wash away the grimy feeling she has on her skin.

But she knows that no matter how much she washes herself, the images of four dead women lying in icy water will cling to her forever.

## CHAPTER 13

The Captain's Table is a quaint little restaurant overlooking Whitby harbour. When Greg and I arrive, Terry and Marcia are already seated and waiting for us. Greg introduces me to Terry, a jovial-looking, balding man in his sixties.

Terry then introduces us both to his wife, a pleasant grey-haired lady who seems to have made much more effort than her husband regarding her appearance. Her hair is delicately pinned up on top of her head, her makeup subtle yet perfect, and her black dress is elegant.

Terry, on the other hand, is wearing a dark green blazer and a cream shirt which could be smart but the shirt is untucked from his trousers and the blazer looks a couple of sizes too small.

I feel a slight pang of guilt for noticing such things. And I'm hardly one who should be passing judgement; I had to squeeze into my best trousers, which I haven't worn in about a year, and my blouse feels tight around the shoulders. Nia's description of me as "curvy" might actually have been a kindness.

We sit and the small talk begins. I smile and nod at the appropriate places and even contribute every now and then. Yes, the weather is bad but it could be worse at this time of year. Of course I wish Greg didn't have to commute an hour each way every day but no, we aren't interested in moving to Middlesbrough. Yes, we've fallen in love with Whitby already and yes, the news regarding "that missing girl" is terrible.

But my attention has been caught by something else. From my seat, I can see the other diners in the restaurant and I find my gaze drawn to a fair-haired woman sitting at a table near the door with a dark-haired teenager. Something about the woman seems familiar but I'm having trouble placing her.

"What do you think, Kate?" Marcia asks, looking in my direction.

I have no idea what she's asking. I lost the train of the conversation a couple of minutes ago.

"Sorry," I say. "Could you repeat that?"

Greg shoots me a look but Marcia seems unfazed and smiles. "Of course. I was just saying that if local restaurants like this one were turned into chains, they'd probably fail because they'd lose their character. What do you think?"

"Oh, yes, I agree. It's the local charm that makes these places so successful. You can't just package that up and ship it all over the country."

Everyone seems satisfied by that answer so I go back to staring at the woman by the door. Where the hell have I seen her before?

Then it hits me. I saw a photograph of her taken only this morning. But in that photo, her hair was scraped back into a pony tail, her hands stuffed into the pockets of her long coat. Now, her hair is worn down, reaching to her shoulders. She's wearing a white sleeveless lace blouse and slim-legged black trousers with a pair of ankle boots. She looks a million miles away from how she looked at the Amy Donovan crime scene.

A waiter comes over to our table and asks if we're ready to order. I haven't even looked at my menu yet but everyone else at the table seems ready so I quickly scan the main dishes and when it comes to my turn, I order the seafood linguine. Terry asks for a bottle of the restaurant's best white wine and the waiter disappears.

I don't know what's wrong with me tonight. My head is all over the place. Well that's a lie. I *do* know what's wrong. Now that I've seen Detective Inspector Summers, I want to ask her what the police were doing at Northmoor House after Stephanie Wilmot went missing. I want to know if there's a reason they questioned everyone in the flats.

Ivy said Rob was out when the police came to the house and that they said they'd return later. What if they never followed up on that? What if they ignored what Ivy told them because she's an old woman and they thought she was being dramatic? It's little, seemingly innocuous mistakes like those that allow people to slip through the net.

*So now you're saying Rob is a murderer?*

I shake my head against my own mental question. I'm not saying he's a murderer, not even thinking such a thing. It's just that if anyone in Northmoor House should be questioned about a missing woman, it's him. What if the police weren't thorough in their investigation? They obviously went to Northmoor House for a reason. I just hope that reason didn't get lost somewhere in the course of the investigation due to laziness or incompetence.

DI Summers gets up from her table and heads for the Ladies loo. This could be my chance to get some answers. I wait a couple of minutes before excusing myself from the table and following her.

When I get inside, she's standing at the sink, washing her hands. She looks at me and smiles but the smile transforms into an expression of wariness when I approach her.

"DI Summers," I say.

"Yes, can I help you?" She shakes water from her hands and pulls a paper towel from the dispenser.

"I'm not sure. My name's Kate Lumley and I live at Northmoor House, a few miles north of town. I was speaking to a neighbour of mine and she told me that the police came around to the house a couple of years ago and questioned the residents regarding a missing woman."

She looks interested. Her eyes search my face and I know she's making an assessment regarding my veracity. "Do you have some information you'd like to pass on to the police regarding the case?"

"No, not exactly. I was just wondering why the police were there. At Northmoor House. Stephanie Wilmot lived miles away. Was there a specific reason the police questioned everyone in the flats?"

She frowns and shakes her head. "No, you're confused. We didn't go to Northmoor House in connection with Stephanie. Like you said, she lived and died twenty miles away. There was no reason for us to question anyone in your building."

She's right; I am confused. Was Ivy mistaken about the police coming round to Northmoor House? She'd seemed so sure, had even provided details of her conversation with them.

"Sorry to have bothered you," I tell DI Summers, turning back to the door.

"You say you live at Northmoor House?" she asks as I'm reaching for the door handle.

I turn to face her. "Yes, we moved there recently."

She seems to be considering something, then lets out a long breath and shrugs to herself. "Okay, what I'm going to tell you is public knowledge that you could find in any newspaper. I wasn't investigating this particular case but it's common knowledge that the police made inquiries at

Northmoor House regarding a missing person. Her name was Caroline Shields."

"So is there a reason the police asked the residents in my building questions about Caroline Shields?"

DI Summers nods. "Yes, there's a very good reason. Before she disappeared, Caroline lived at Northmoor House. In the top floor flat."

## CHAPTER 14

I feel like I've been punched in the gut. A woman went missing from our flat? It suddenly feels as if the floor is tipping away from me and I'm in danger of falling over. I lean on the sink and try to catch my breath.

"Are you all right?' DI Summers asks.

"Yes, I'm fine. I just...never knew."

"Listen," she says coming closer to me and putting a steadying hand on my shoulder. "If it's any consolation, it was two years ago and Caroline didn't actually disappear from the flat. Her car was found abandoned on the moors."

"So you think she was killed on the moors like those other women?"

"I can't discuss that."

"Did you question the landlord at Northmoor House? Rob North? My neighbour said he was out when the police came. Did they come back later to question him?"

"I can't discuss that either. And as I said, I wasn't involved in the investigation. Look, I'm sorry to be the bearer of shocking news but I have to get back to my table now. My daughter is waiting for me."

"Yes, of course. I'm sorry."

"There's no need to be sorry, Kate. I can see how this could be a shock to you. But Caroline's disappearance is in the past. You mustn't let it affect you."

I nod but say nothing. She pats me on the shoulder gently and leaves the Ladies.

I remain leaning on the sink, my legs shaky, my mind racing. If Caroline disappeared from our flat, and if someone abducted her, wouldn't it likely be someone who saw her every day? Who knew her? Surely the police would have investigated that angle.

I don't know any of the answers. The questions repeat themselves over and over in my head, niggling at my thoughts. Did someone abduct Caroline and get away with it?

I need to find more facts regarding the case but I'm also aware how much time I've been in the Ladies. Marcia will probably come looking for me soon. I check myself in the mirror and try to compose myself. I can look up Caroline Shields later; for now, I have to make small talk and pretend everything's fine. It's important to Greg.

But everything isn't fine. My head is still swirling with questions as I go back to the table. Everyone is waiting for me, ready to start their meals, which have been delivered to the table already. I take my seat and force myself to smile. "Mmm, this looks good."

Terry pours a glass of wine for everyone and makes a toast to new friendships. As we clink our glasses, I look over to the DI's table. She's eating a fish stew and talking to her daughter. She doesn't glance in my direction.

As far as she's concerned, the fact that Caroline lived in my flat when she disappeared is nothing for me to worry about.

But the police aren't infallible. They don't know everything. They didn't know for sure what happened to Danny Coates. They didn't know exactly what happened to Max.

I sip my wine. Greg makes another toast.

"Here's to the success of the bank and a profitable future."

We clink glasses again. But when I take a second sip of my wine, I'm not drinking to the bank or its future. I'm drinking to my own, unspoken, toast. *Here's to finding out what really happened to Caroline Shields.*

## CHAPTER 15

My phone wakes me up the following morning. I reach for it on the bedside table and have to feel around for it before I finally find it. Bleary-eyed, I check the name on the screen before answering. Nia.

"Morning, Nia," I say, my voice thick. How much did I drink last night? I remember having two glasses of wine and then Terry ordering another bottle. My mind had been wandering so much that I hadn't watched how much I was drinking. Greg also had a few too many and we left the car at the marina car park and got a taxi home.

"Sounds like someone had a late night," Nia says. "Are you still in bed? You know it's nearly eleven, right?"

"Is it?" I sit up and check the bedside clock. Nia's right; I've slept most of the morning away. And I still have to go into town to get the car. I let out a low groan. I need coffee.

Nia laughs. "Well I hope your night was worth it. Did you have a good time?"

"Yes, we went out with Greg's boss and his wife."

"Nice," she says. "So Greg is schmoozing his way to the top, huh?"

"No, apparently the boss takes out all new members of staff."

"Did he pay for all your drinks?"

"Yes."

"Nice."

I slide out of bed and pad to the kitchen. I fill the coffee maker and lean on the counter while I wait for it to do its thing.

"I was wondering if I could take you up on your offer," Nia says.

"Offer?"

"To look after the kids for a night. If it's not convenient, I can—"

"No, no, it's fine. We'd love to have them. When were you thinking?"

"How about Saturday night?"

That gives me a couple of days to get the spare room ready. At the moment, it's full of boxes we haven't unpacked yet but we need to get on with that and needing the room for Nia's kids on the weekend will be a good impetus. "Yeah, that's great."

"Awesome. I'm going to book a secluded B&B somewhere. Maybe Will and I just need to reconnect, you know?"

"I'm sure it's nothing more serious than that, Nia."

There's a pause, then a sigh, and then she says, "I hope you're right."

"Do you want me to collect them from yours on Saturday?"

"No, you're doing me enough of a favour as it is. I'll bring them over to you. I've got your new address. How does lunchtime sound?"

"Sounds great."

"See you then. Can't wait to see your lovely new flat." She hangs up.

I toss my phone on the counter and look around the kitchen. The flat doesn't feel so lovely at the moment. I can't stop thinking about Caroline Shields. This kitchen is where she used to drink her morning coffee, unaware that her mornings were numbered. How long had she lived here before she disappeared?

The only person I can ask won't be able to remember details like that. Ivy might be able to remember *something* about Caroline, though, even if it's something insignificant. I want to know what Caroline was like, what kind of person she was, before I go online and look up the facts surrounding her case. Even though I never knew her, she lived here, in this space where I now live, and that makes me feel close to her. I want her to be more than just a name in an emotionless news report.

I pour a mug of coffee and drink it at the window, looking out towards the distant cliffs and sea. A dusting of snow lies over everything like a layer of dandruff and there are more tiny flakes in the air, floating on the breeze. The snow reminds me of the leak in the kitchen ceiling last night. I go in there and check it.

There's a damp stain but no more water dripping down. Rob must have fixed it. He didn't answer when we were on our way out to the Captain's Table last night so Greg came back upstairs, wrote a note, and taped it to the landlord's door.

He must have read it because the leak has stopped.

For now anyway.

I get dressed, take a couple of painkillers for the headache that's been throbbing in the back of my head and threatening to get worse if I don't do something about it, and go down to Ivy's.

Her door is open and Winston is roaming the hallway. He ignores me today, more interested in sniffing the door to the parking area than in greeting me.

Ivy, on the other hand, beams when she sees me. She's standing at the door watching the cat, probably worried that he's going to go out in the snow. "Hello, dear. Fancy a cuppa?"

"That would be lovely," I say.

"Come in, then." She goes into the kitchen and starts fussing over the tea pot and cups.

I follow her and take a seat at the kitchen table. "Ivy, do you remember a woman who lived in the upstairs flat before Greg and I moved in? Her name was Caroline."

She ponders that for a moment, frowning with concentration. "Caroline? It doesn't ring a bell, dear."

I'm not surprised. I'm sure Ivy can't remember

my name either. Adding that detail has probably confused her. "Well never mind her name. The woman who used to live on the top floor."

"Oh yes, I remember her. Lovely girl, she was." She pours water from the kettle into the pot. "Caroline, was that her name? I'm sorry, dear, I can't remember if that was her name or not."

"That was her name," I tell her. "But that isn't important. Did you ever speak to her?"

"Plenty of times," she says, bringing the pot to the table. "She used to buy little bags of treats for Winston. He loved them and he loved her. He used to purr every time he saw her." She knits her brows. "Caroline. Yes, that *was* her name, now I come to think about it."

"She sounds nice," I say, waiting to see if Ivy will provide any more information unprompted.

"She always said hello," Ivy says after a moment. "Always cheery. She never had a bad word to say about anyone."

"Not even Rob?" I ask.

Her face darkens. "No, not even him. I saw the way he looked at her, though. I knew what he was thinking." She taps the side of her head. "The same thing that goes through the minds of most men when they see a pretty girl."

"Do you think he fancied her?"

"No doubt about it. I caught him snooping around her car one day. I went out to call Winston in and there was Rob, looking into her car windows. God only knows what he was up to. I said, 'Get away from there, you, before I give you a good hiding.' He scarpered pretty quickly, I can tell you."

I remember the footprints in the snow leading from the back door of the house to my car.

"Caroline was oblivious, though. She thought he was harmless enough. The only time I saw them have harsh words was one time when she came down here and accused him of stealing her pencil case. She said nobody else had a key to the flat and there hadn't been a break-in so he must have gone in there and taken it."

"What happened?"

"He denied it, of course. He said, 'What would I want with a stupid bloody Disney pencil case?' That sent her into a bit of a spin. She said, 'How would you know it's a Disney one if you didn't take it?' She was clever, you see."

"What did he say to that?" I ask, thinking of my missing pen.

"He told her that just about everything she

owned was Disney so it was a lucky guess. He was right about that. She loved Disney princesses, even at her age. She had a handbag, purse, umbrella, the whole lot. She even dressed up as Snow White for a Christmas party. Looked lovely, she did."

She pours the tea. "Anyway, I told her to go to the police but she didn't. I'm not sure they'd have done anything about it anyway. They don't even come out if your car's been stolen these days, never mind a pencil case."

"When the police came—" I begin.

"They didn't come, dear. I told you, they wouldn't come out for a missing pencil case."

"No, I mean when they came later, after Caroline had gone missing. You said Rob was out."

"That's right. I told them, 'He's a dodgy one, him across the corridor.' They didn't seem interested. Even when I offered to let them into his flat they didn't want to know. Would Hercule Poirot have refused to look around a suspect's flat? No, he'd have snooped around and found some clues."

"Did they come back later? When Rob was in?"

She thinks for a moment and then shakes her head. "No, dear, they only came once. I never saw them again after that."

*So Rob wasn't interviewed by the police regarding*

*Caroline's disappearance.* That seems like a huge oversight considering he lived in the same building.

"Terrible thing, it was, that poor girl going missing like that," Ivy says.

A thought strikes me. "What happend to all her stuff? In the flat, I mean. She must have had furniture and belongings."

"Removal men came and took it all away," she says. "This was some time after she disappeared. I think they were sent here by her parents. They probably couldn't face coming here themselves, poor things."

"And did anyone else move in after that?"

"Not until you and your husband came. Rob redecorated the flat after it was empty and you know how slow he is to get off his arse and get to work. Took him almost two years to get it done. Two years of banging and clattering, sawing and hammering. I thought I was going to go crazy with all that noise. I had to turn the telly right up just so I could hear my stories. And poor Winston was frightened out of his wits."

"I'll bet he was." I wonder what Rob was doing up there that required hammering and sawing. Redecorating shouldn't involve much more than putting a lick of paint on the walls. Was the flat different before we moved in? Has he remodelled it? I have no way of knowing without seeing pictures of how it looked before.

"Anyway, that's all in the past now," Ivy says. "Now you're here. How are you settling in? Did you go out somewhere nice last night?"

"You heard us go out?"

She taps her ear. "I told you, I don't miss anything, me. And I saw that note you left on Rob's door. I can't believe that after all that work he must have done up there, the attic's leaking. Shoddy workmanship, you see. You can't expect much more from him."

"Well I think he fixed it last night."

"Did he? I heard him go up there. He takes the lift, you see. Very noisy. But I didn't hear any banging or anything. Not that I want to hear any more after two years of it."

"Well it's not leaking this morning."

"If I were you, I'd go up there myself and check. You can't trust him to do anything properly."

"I can't go up there," I tell her. "He's locked the attic."

"What did he do that for?"

I shrug. "Greg was going to go up there and

Rob stopped him. The next day, there was a padlock on the hatch."

"Silly bugger. Anyone would think he's got the crown jewels up there."

I finish my tea and remember my car. "Ivy, it's been nice chatting but I've got to go. My car is parked in town. I'm going to go down there and get it."

She looks a little disappointed. "All right, dear. You be careful out there."

"I will. See you later." I go out through the open door and ascend the stairs to my flat, where I don my jacket and other cold weather gear. As I go back down to the ground floor, I search for the number of a local taxi company on my phone.

Just before I reach the bottom of the stairs, a voice from behind me startles me. "Hi, Kate."

I turn to see Mike, the tenant from the first floor. He's also wearing a jacket and a hat and looks like he's also on his way out.

"Hi," I say, moving aside so he can get past me. I'm probably slowing him up by sauntering down the stairs and consulting my phone at the same time.

He does move past me but then stops and turns to face me. "You going out?"

"Yeah, I'm going into town." I find a website for a taxi company and scroll through it, looking for their phone number.

"Want a lift?" he asks.

I look up from the phone, unsure what to say. He's a total stranger, after all. But he's also my neighbour.

"It's just that I noticed your car isn't outside," he says.

"It's at the car park in town. I was just going to get a taxi."

"No need for that. I'm going into town myself. Come on, I'll drop you off." He walks ahead of me to the exit door.

"Hang on," I say, stopping at Ivy's door. While he waits for me, I shout to Ivy. "Ivy, I'm just going into town with Mike from upstairs. He's giving me a lift. Is there anything you need?"

"No, thank you, dear. Have a nice time."

Now, Mike knows that Ivy is aware of where I'm going and who with. Probably over-cautious on my part but you can't be too careful these days.

I follow him outside to the red Volvo I've seen parked out here before. "Get in," he offers, indicating the passenger side.

When I'm seated and putting my seatbelt on,

he slides into the driver's seat. "Which car park are we going to?"

"The one at the marina if that's all right."

"Of coure." When he starts the car, the radio comes on, blaring out high volume pop music. "Sorry," Mike says, turning it down to a barely audible level. "That's the music that keeps me awake while I'm commuting to and from work."

"What do you do?" I ask.

"I work for a software development company in York."

"That's a bit of a commute."

"Well, luckily the company I work for is based on this side of the city so it only takes me about an hour each way." He steers the Volvo around Rob's Land Rover and out of the parking area onto the road. "Anyway, it's a nice drive over the moors. I just relax and take in the scenery."

"And listen to loud pop music."

He grins. "Yeah, that too."

"Have you lived at Northmoor House long?"

"A few years. I love the location. Most people would move closer to work, I suppose, but I like to have that separation. The moors are like a barrier between me and my work life."

I nod.

"The flat is great," he continues. "The only drawback is the landlord. He's a bit of a tool."

I don't give anything away. Keeping my voice light and inquisitive, I ask, "Really? Why do you say that?"

"He never gets anything done around the place. The house is a lovely Victorian building that needs attention and the guy in charge of its upkeep is just lazy."

"Ivy was just telling me that he's been working on it constantly for the past two years."

Mike shakes his head. "No, I wouldn't say that. He might have dabbed some paint here and there but that's about it. He's totally useless."

"Maybe someone should tell his parents," I say, remembering Greg's threat to write them a letter complaining about their son's job performance.

"They won't listen," Mike says.

"I'm sure they'd want to know if their lovely Victorian house is falling apart due to their son's negligence."

"Trust me," he says. "They don't care." He turns onto the road that leads into Whitby and says, "Anyway, what about you? What do you do?"

"I'm a book editor."

"Wow, that sounds interesting. So you decide which books are going to be on the shelves?"

"Well, I decide which books my employers should publish. And then I work with the publisher and author to get the book to as high a standard as possible before publication."

"Sounds interesting. I'm quite an avid reader myself, actually."

"Oh? What genre?"

"Nordic Noir mostly. You know, Henning Mankell and Jussi Adler-Olsen, things like that."

"Ah, you like crime fiction."

He nods. "I do. I admit it. Do you work on any of that kind of stuff?"

"Sometimes but I mainly work on historical and gothic romances."

We're almost in town now. Mike guides the Volvo along the road that leads to the marina. A few people have braved the weather and are walking along the pavement, huddled in thick jackets and coats against the cold and the fluttering flakes of snow.

"Here we are," Mike says, pulling into the car park. "Marina car park. And your Mini looks safe and sound, if a little snow-covered."

My car is parked a couple of spaces away, covered with a light dusting of white.

"Yes, I hope this weather lets up soon," I say.

"Not yet," he replies. "We're in for some heavy weather next week."

"Thanks for the lift," I say, climbing out of the car.

"Anytime." He leans across the passenger seat I just vacated and gives me a brief wave. "Have a good day."

I close the door and head over to my Mini. There's nothing I need in town so I might as well head straight home and get on the computer. I need to get some work done but I also want to look up the details surrounding Caroline Shields' disappearance.

When I get back to Northmoor House, the snow is coming down more determinedly. I rush inside and shake myself off in the hallway, watched by an amused-looking Winston. I give Ivy a wave through her open door and head up to my flat.

The first thing I do is check the ceiling over the kitchen sink. If the leak hasn't been fixed properly, then this snow would surely be getting into the attic and leaking down into our flat. Everything looks exactly as it did this morning. I breathe out a sigh of relief. That's one problem solved.

I leave the kitchen and look around the living room, paying particular attention to my desk area. Nothing seems out of place or missing. My pen, which has come from the same pack as the missing one, is sitting on top of my notebook.

As far as I can tell, no one has been in here while I was out.

I boot up the computer and type Caroline Shields' name into the search engine. A number of hits appear, mainly from various news outlets. They all tell me the same thing: Caroline Shields, 23, disappeared on the 17th of December, 2017. Her car was later found abandoned on the moors. She was due to attend a Christmas party in Scarborough that night but seemed to have been driving in the opposite direction, heading north of Whitby instead of south.

That was scant information to go on. I search through a few more articles, trying to find more details. I finally find something to add to the facts, a paragraph on the Sun's website that surprises me because it mentions Ivy:

*According to Caroline's neighbour Ivy Rose— possibly the last person to see Caroline alive—Caroline was looking forward to attending a Christmas party and was making plans for the coming new year. There was no indication that she was depressed in any way or might have taken her own life.*

I had no idea that Ivy was the last person to see Caroline alive. Maybe something Caroline said to her could be an important clue. Of course, Ivy probably wouldn't remember much about it now and the police would have already questioned her about those kinds of details at the time.

Wouldn't they?

They didn't come back and interview Rob North so they might have missed other things as well.

I find some pictures of Caroline. She's pretty, with long blonde hair, blue eyes, and a face that looks younger than her 23 years.

And now she's missing, maybe buried somewhere on the moors. She might never be discovered and her parents and friends will go to their own graves having no idea what happened to her.

There's such a dearth of information regarding Caroline on the Net that I seem to have reached the limit of my online search. The only option I have is to see if Ivy remembers anything else about her. I suppose I could ask Mike but I barely know him and he might wonder why I'm asking.

Unsure as to my next move regarding Caroline, I open the *Secrets of Falcon House* manuscript and get to work. I might as well do something productive and I have a deadline to meet.

As I read, the book's heroine discovers that her employer, the dashing Mr Cornwall, has murdered his wife and buried her body beneath the folly. Before Cornwall has a chance to kill the heroine and cover up his crime, she flees straight into the arms of Douglas Trevelyan, the local chief of police.

Trevelyan arrests Cornwall, the wife's body is taken as evidence, and Cornwall admits his crime, ensuring that he'll face the hangman's noose.

I sigh wistfully. At least someone is able to solve the mysteries that surround her and see justice done.

# CHAPTER 16

Dani arrives at headquarters to find the post-mortem report on Amy Donovan sitting on her desk. She reads it thoroughly but it doesn't tell her anything she hadn't already guessed. There were no signs of a struggle because, like the other women, Amy had been injected with a solution of diazepam suspended in saline. The injection was administered into her trapezius muscle. Death was due to drowning in the body of water in which she'd been found.

The report tells Dani nothing new, nothing helpful.

The forensic report is just as unhelpful. Rickman's team has taken particles from the water and the grass in the area where Amy was found but apart from dog hairs and a couple of fibres that don't match any of the fibres from the other crime scenes, there's nothing earth-shattering, no clue that breaks the case open.

She looks up to see Matt Flowers approaching her desk with two mugs of coffee. He puts one in front of her.

"Thanks, Matt. Please tell me you have some good news regarding this case."

"Afraid not, Guv."

Dani slides the post-mortem report across the desk towards him. "Pull up a chair and read this."

He does so, grabbing a spare chair from the next desk and poring over the report with an intense focus. When he's done, he closes the folder and says, "Same as all the others. He drugs them and then drowns them."

"Do you think he adds the red ribbon before he drowns them or after they're dead?"

Matt shrugs. "Does is make a difference?"

She lets out a sigh. "Probably not. I just want to know every detail, no matter how small. What goes through his mind when he drowns them? Who do they remind him of after he's added the ribbon?"

"Do you think he visits them later?" Matt asks. "Maybe he goes back again and again."

"Maybe. That would be consistent with a lot of killers' behaviour. And we always find them just as a thaw begins. Before that, they're probably lying under a layer of ice for a few days."

"Like a butterfly under glass," Matt says.

Dani nods. "Yeah, he must visit them, admire his own handiwork. For him, it's all about the visual he creates. So I'd say he goes back again and again to look at his creation."

She swallows some of the coffee and says, "Andrew Thomas, the dog walker who found her. Did he see anyone hanging around in that area on any of the days previous to discovering the body?"

"No, Guv. He doesn't always walk the dog at the same location. Said he hasn't been to that particular spot in quite a while."

"Has anybody else been up there recently? Hikers? Locals?"

"We've put up posters in the area and we're inquiring at the local villages, B&Bs, and hotels. A walking group from Leeds was up there the day after Amy went missing and a couple of the members recall seeing a green Land Rover Defender parked by the side of the road but no one remembers the registration or any distinguishing marks on the vehicle."

"What about any photos they took while they were out walking? Have you checked those? They might have inadvertently snapped a picture of the vehicle."

"I'll get on that. Is that all, Guv?"

"Yes. Let me know if any of those photos give us a look a that Land Rover." It's a long shot, she knows, but every lead has to be chased down and sometimes the most innocuous detail can turn out to be the one piece of the puzzle that reveals the whole picture.

"Oh, just one more thing," she says to Matt as he's wheeling the chair back to the desk from which he got it.

"Guv?"

"The Caroline Shields case. Who questioned the other residents at the building where she lived?"

His brow creases for a second as he tries to recall the details. "A couple of uniforms, I think, Guv. It wasn't our case. DI Henson was in charge of that one."

"Do you know if they questioned the landlord?"

Matt shrugs. "Not without checking the case file."

"Thanks, I'll have a look at it myself later."

"Do you think they missed something?"

"I don't know," she admits, remembering what the woman in the toilets at the Captain's Table told her. "It might be nothing."

He walks away, leaving Dani to ponder the possibility that a mistake has been made.

It isn't likely that Henson would miss something so obvious as questioning someone who lived in the same building as Caroline but Dani needs to check that an oversight hasn't occurred for her own peace of mind. If Henson was still here, she'd ask him but he transferred to the Met last year and since his departure, along with a lack of evidence, clues, or leads, the Caroline Shields case has languished.

Could the case finally be solved by something a woman in a seafood restaurant toilet mentioned to her? It seems unlikely but still worth checking into.

She reaches into her handbag and retrieves the Captain's Table napkin she hastily scribbled on after her encounter with the woman in the toilets. She remembers exactly what the woman said to her and doesn't need the *aide memoire* but refers to it anyway just to make sure.

There are six words written on the napkin.

*Kate Lumley*

*Northmoor House*

*Rob North*

Dani does a quick Internet search for "Kate Lumley" and groans when she sees the long list of results.

*Journalist Falsely Accuses Man of Murdering Own Child*

*Manchester Recorder Journalist Sacked After False Accusations*

She vaguely remembers the story. Didn't some woman believe her son had been killed by her husband and a journalist published a story shaming him even though all the evidence said the child had drowned in a stream?

"Don't tell me she's the bloody journalist," Dani whispers to herself as she clicks on some of the links. The story is exactly as she remembers it and most of the articles carry a picture of Kate Lumley, the same woman who'd approached her in the Captain's Table toilets last night and asked if the police had questioned the landlord at Northmoor House.

Dani sighs. "She's the bloody journalist."

This doesn't mean Kate's inquiry about Rob North should be discounted, of course, but now Dani is disappointed. What might have been a promising lead in the Caroline Shields case is probably nothing more than a deluded journalist's fantasy. Maybe she's trying to atone for past sins by finding an actual murderer to balance out the fact that she falsely accused someone in the past.

But how accurate is she this time?

She looks up and sees Matt hovering by her desk. When she acknowledges him, he holds up a thick binder and places it on her desk. "Caroline Shields' case file, Guv, including all the information on the inquiries carried out at Northmoor House."

"Thanks, Matt," Dani says, reaching for the file. "You read my mind."

CHAPTER 17

When Saturday arrives, I'm still none the wiser regarding Caroline Shields. Over the past couple of days, I've been finding out as much as I can about Caroline by searching online and casually dropping questions in conversations with Ivy.

Neither method has got me anywhere. There's hardly anything on the Net and Ivy can't seem to remember anything important. She can tell you what Winston had for dinner three weeks ago but can't remember much about a young woman who vanished from the flat two floors above.

I know Ivy isn't to blame for that but it's frustrating when I'm trying to piece together information for my investigation.

If I had something to go on, some lead that

tells me where to look next, I might be able to try and find out what happened to Caroline Shields. As it is, I've come to a dead end.

I'm sitting by the window, watching the sun glimmer off the last vestige of snow as it melts away, when Nia's white Nissan pulls up beside the house. "They're here," I tell Greg, getting up from my seat and going to the door.

Greg pops his head out of the kitchen. He's been baking potato smiley faces which he says will be, "Better for them than that store-bought rubbish," and the entire flat smells like a chip shop.

Leaving him to it, I go downstairs and greet the Mitchell family at the front door.

"Hey," Nia says, coming up to me and giving me a hug while Will unloads two suitcases from the back of the Nissan.

Jordan and Kishawn stand just behind their mother. Kishawn looks more grown up than I remember her. Even though she's only nine, there are hints of the woman she will become in her face, which seems to have acquired a sense of maturity and a confident look in her brown eyes. She's dressed in jeans and a faded grey hoodie that has the word *Glamour* in gold lettering across the front.

Jordan is also wearing jeans and a dark blue woollen jumper. When he smiles at me, I see that he has a front tooth missing.

"What happened to your tooth, Jordan?" I ask him.

"I fell."

"Oh dear."

"He fell off the climbing frame at school," Nia tells me as they follow me into the house.

"A lift!" Jordan says delightedly, running to the end of the hallway. He turns to his mother and puts on a pleading face. "Please can we go in the lift?"

"If that's all right with Kate," Nia says.

"Sure, knock yourself out. But there's only room for two people."

"I'll take him up," Will says. "Since I have the suitcases."

Jordan and his dad get into the lift while Nia, Kishawn, and I climb up the stairs. When we reach the first floor, Mike is approaching the stairs, carrying a black bin bag. When he sees us, he smiles and steps back to let us pass. "After you, ladies."

"Thanks, Mike," I say as we pass him and

ascend the next flight of stairs.

"Who's he?" Nias asks when we get to the second floor. "He's cute."

"The downstairs neighbour. Mike has the first floor, and Ivy is on the ground floor. Rob, the landlord, lives in the basement flat."

"It's a big place," Nia observes, looking around at the wide hallway. "I don't think much to the lift, though." We can hear it trundling up from below but it hasn't reached our floor yet.

"I never use it," I tell her. "Too slow."

When the lift finally arrives, Will pushes the gate open and emerges with Jordan and suitcases.

Greg appears at the flat door, still wearing the dark blue apron he wears when he's cooking. "Hey, guys. Come in, come in."

Everyone goes into the flat and I hear Nia exclaim, Wow, this is lovely!" but I'm still staring at the lift. I'm remembering when Rob came up to stop Greg going into the attic. We'd barely been out in the hallway more than 20 seconds when the lift arrived at this floor.

But it's so slow that even if Rob had seen us on the hallway camera, as Greg suggested, and got into the lift immediately, he wouldn't have arrived at this floor so quickly. The lift takes at least a minute to travel here from the ground floor.

So Rob must have already been in the lift before we went out into the hallway. How could he have known we were going to go into the attic before we even left the flat?

Greg pops his head around the door. "You coming?"

"Yeah," I say, turning away from the lift and going into the flat. Nia and Will are making all the right noises about our new home and the kids are exploring it with interest.

"This place is lovely," Nia says, coming up to me. "And the views are magnificent!"

I smile and nod but I'm distracted, my eyes searching the walls and ceiling for any cracks or holes.

Anywhere a camera might be hidden.

## CHAPTER 18

It's cold and windy on the beach and my scarf is blowing about crazily, whipping my face, but Jordan and Kishawn are having a great time splashing in the sea in their wellies and chasing each other across the sand.

Greg and I wander along behind them, arm in arm, and I wonder if this is what it might be like in the future if we have children of our own; lazy afternoons on the beach while they play and run without a care in the world.

My earlier worries about a camera in our flat have been assuaged. A quick inspection of the walls and ceiling revealed nowhere that such a device could be hidden.

In fact, it looks like any holes in the plaster

have been recently filled and given a lick of paint. So Rob might not have spent the two years after Caroline's disappearance remodelling the flat, as Ivy suggested, but he's certainly dabbed some paint here and there, like Mike said.

"I hope Nia and Will are having a nice time," I say to Greg.

"I'm sure they are. Who wouldn't want to be in an isolated B&B in the middle of winter? "

"They just want to spend some time together. So isolated is perfect."

He shrugs. "It just seems like an odd time of the year."

"Nia's a bit worried that things aren't going great between them at the moment so there's no time like the present to get it sorted. Besides, it's a new year, so why not also a new phase of their relationship? It's a perfect time."

"I didn't realise they were having problems. Will hasn't mentioned anything to me."

"Well, women talk more about that sort of thing to their friends, I suppose."

"Whereas men have a stiff upper lip and carry on regardless."

"No, men bottle everything up and worry about

it without saying anything to anyone and then have a heart attack in their fifties."

"Hmm, I suppose so."

We walk on a bit farther and I watch the seagulls hovering above the waves and standing by the sea's edge, hoping a tasty morsel will be washed up somewhere close by. Jordan runs up to one but the bird takes flight long before he reaches it and chastises him with a loud cry.

"I wonder how many times Caroline Shields came to the beach?" I wonder aloud.

"You're still thinking about her?"

I told Greg about Caroline going missing two years ago and the fact that she lived in our flat and was friends with Ivy. I also told him about the police not interviewing Rob North when they came to the house. Greg agrees that it's an oversight but doesn't think much of it. "It's not like he's a murderer," he said when I mentioned it to him.

I didn't take the conversation any further. After the trouble we had following the Simon Coates debacle, I don't want Greg to think I'm going to throw accusations at someone else.

And I'm *not* going to throw any accusations around. Not without proof, anyway.

"I just wonder about her life sometimes, that's all," I tell Greg. "And some things make me think about her. Like being on this beach. How many times did Caroline come here, not knowing that her days were numbered?"

"Sounds a bit morbid."

"I know but I can't help feeling that way sometimes with all that's going on around us. They found Amy Donovan quite close to where we live."

"Okay, but you don't even know if Caroline Shields is dead. For all you know, she could have faked her death and now she's living it up in the Bahamas or somewhere like that."

"I'm sure that isn't what happened, Greg."

"Why not? You couldn't blame her if she *did* run off to warmer climes. It's bloody freezing here. And we're supposed to get another snowstorm in a few days, as well as sub-zero temperatures."

"She didn't run off; her car was found on the moors."

"Well, that's easily explained." He thinks for a couple of seconds and then says, "She ran away with her lover. They drove out to the moors together, dumped Caroline's car, and then drove to the airport in the lover's car. And that car is still in the long-stay car park at the airport."

"After two years?"

"Well it is long-stay after all."

"And did Caroline change her clothes before boarding the flight or did she arrive in the Bahamas dressed as Snow White?"

Now he looks confused. "What?"

"She was on her way to a Christmas party that night, dressed as Snow White."

He considers that for a moment and then says, "She stayed in costume and her lover was dressed as Grumpy the dwarf."

I laugh. "You've got an overactive imagination."

"I'm not the one thinking our landlord has something to do with a vanished woman."

"I never said that."

"No, but you're thinking it, aren't you? That's why you mentioned the police not interviewing Rob. Why would that be an issue unless you think there's some reason why they *should* have interviewed him?"

"I just mentioned it as an example of how sloppy the police investigation was, that's all."

"Come on, Kate, I know you better than that."

I shrug.

"Look," he says, "Rob is creepy, and rude, and lacks social skills, but that doesn't make him a murderer or whatever it is you're accusing him of."

"I know that. I'm just—" I let my words trail off.

"You're trying to solve the case of Caroline Shields' disappearance. Just like you tried to solve the case of Danny Coates' death. You can't solve the world's problems, Kate."

"I'm not trying to."

"You are. You always do."

"I'm just trying to make sure that if a person hurts someone else, they don't get away with it."

"That's the purpose of the police. They investigate crimes and put bad guys away. You told the policewoman at the restaurant about them not interviewing Rob so if she thinks that's relevant, I'm sure she'll follow it up. If not, then she won't. But that's for her to decide because that's her job."

"Whereas I'm just a lowly book editor who shouldn't get involved in such things, is that right?"

"I didn't say that."

"You didn't have to."

"I just don't want you doing something—" Now it's his turn to let his words trail off.

"Something stupid?"

"I didn't say that either."

I let out a long breath. "You didn't have to,

Greg. Don't worry, we're not going to have a repeat of what happened last year."

He doesn't say anything to that. We walk on in silence, watching Jordan and Kishawn as they chase seagulls and pick up pebbles that have been worn down by the relentless sea for so long that they've lost their original shape and all that remains is a smooth remnant of what they once were.

When we arrive back at Northmoor House, we're all tired. Jordan is almost asleep on the back seat and Kishawn is typing on her phone and yawning. Greg seems weary as he pulls into the parking area and I feel as if the wind has battered me into an exhausted submission.

"Can I watch telly when we get inside?" Kishawn asks, looking up from her phone.

"Of course," Greg says. "And while you do that, I'm going to make us pasta for tea. Maybe Jordan can help me."

Jordan gives him a tired smile.

Greg grins. "I'll take that as a yes."

We go inside to find Ivy's and Rob's doors both open. Ivy is standing in the hallway with a tin of tuna in her hand. She's looking towards Rob's flat and doesn't seem to have noticed our presence.

"What's up, Ivy?" I touch her gently on the shoulder and she jumps.

"Oh, it's you, dear. It's Winston. He's gone into the basement flat and I can't go in there to get him because of the steps."

"Who's Winston?" Jordan asks.

"Winston is my kitty, dear."

I look at the open door to the basement flat, then back at Ivy. "Where's Rob?"

She shakes her head. "Who knows? He went up in the lift about half an hour ago and left his bloody door open. And Winston, being a curious cat, went down there to have a look around."

"I want to see the kitty!" Jordan says, running towards Rob's door.

"Jordan, come back!" I shout after him but it's too late. He's gone through the door and down the steps to the basement flat.

"I'll get him," Greg says, starting after Jordan.

"No, let me." I push past him. If I want to get a look inside Rob's flat, this is as good a chance as I'm ever going to get. He can hardly get angry if I've gone in there to rescue a child and a cat.

"Don't forget Winston," Ivy calls after me as I go through the door and descend the steps.

The room at the bottom of the steps smells of

unwashed socks and stale food. Because the room is subterranean, the only natural light comes through thin windows set high into the walls. The room is dim and I suppose it has to be lit with artificial light all the time. That, along with the fact that Rob only seems to go out at night, explains why his skin is so pasty.

Jordan is standing in the middle of the room, facing me, fists clenched. His face has a worried expression and he seems to have suddenly thought better of coming down here into the weakly-lit room.

"Jordan, come on!" I wave him over and he comes to me. "Go back upstairs to Greg and Kishawn," I tell him. He does so.

I continue into the flat, calling Winston while I look around the living room.

The furniture in here looks like it's from the '70s. There's a worn green settee with scratched wooden arms and an oval-shaped wooden coffee table with spindly legs. It's weighed down by stacks of magazines. Sitting on a second coffee table which has been repurposed as a TV stand, a large flatscreen TV faces the settee. Beneath this coffee table sit a number of game consoles and an assortment of controllers.

There are posters everywhere, of characters from video games, women from men's magazines, and fantasy art that depicts heavily-muscled barbarians and scantily-clad damsels. A number of horror and science fiction film posters also fight for wall space.

There's a small cluttered and dirty kitchen through an open doorway and two closed doors, which I assume lead to Rob's bedroom and the bathroom. A clatter from the kitchen catches my attention and I turn to see Winston walking across the worktop, sniffing around the pots and pans that are stacked in the sink.

"Winston!"

The cat looks at me and jumps down to the floor. Before I can grab him, he shoots out of the flat and up the stairs to the hallway. I hear Ivy say, "Winston, you naughty boy!"

Then I hear a rumble in the walls and realise it's the lift coming down to the ground floor. My eyes dart around the flat. The lift takes 30 seconds between floors, which means it will take a minute if it's coming from the 2nd floor but only half that if it's coming from the 1st. I can't think of any reason why Rob would be on our floor so I have to assume I only have 30 seconds to look around.

I open one of the doors and enter a small bedroom. As well as an unmade single bed, there's a desk and computer in here, as well as an old wardrobe and a bedside table. The walls in here are covered by posters, like the living room. All of these are photographs or cartoon depictions of women.

There's a small, flat box on the bedside table and I read it without picking it up. The printing on the box says, *Valium (diazepam) 10 mg.*

No wonder Rob is so slow and doesn't do anything in a hurry; he's probably dosing himself with sedatives all the time.

I can't stay in here any longer. The lift is still rumbling but I know it will stop any second now and I can't use the excuse of children or cats to explain why I'm in here when Jordan and Winston are now in the hallway.

I rush out of the bedroom and across the living room to the steps. I take a last look at the flat and notice something on the coffee table, among the piles of magazines.

My bloody pen.

It's too generic an item to be sure but I'm convinced this is the pen I used when I was working on *The Secrets of Falcon House*. And now it's here, sitting on Rob's coffee table, giving me all the confirmation I need that he let himself into our flat while I was out.

Leaving it there, I bound up the steps and out into the hallway where everyone is waiting for me.

"What took you so long?" Greg asks.

"Nothing," I say breathlessly.

The lift judders to a halt and Rob steps out. He sees us standing by his door and his face instantly takes on a suspicious expression. "What's going on?"

"My poor Winston got lost in your flat," Ivy tells him. "You need to keep your door shut in future. God only knows what could have happened to him down there."

Rob looks at his open door and then at each of us in turn. "Well, you know what they say. Curiosity killed the cat."

"Don't you threaten Winston," Ivy shouts at him. "I'll give you a good hiding if you go anywhere near him."

Rob just smiles and disappears through his door, closing it behind him.

"He's a monster," Ivy says. "Threatening a poor defenceless cat like that!"

"I'm sure it's all just for show," Greg tell her. "I don't think he'd actually harm Winston."

I'm not so sure of that but I don't say anything.

Ivy is still incensed. "I meant what I said. If he harms a hair on Winston's head, he'll rue the day, believe me."

"I believe you," Greg says. "I feel sorry for anyone who crosses you, Ivy."

"Just as long as he knows it," she says, pointing at Rob's door.

"I'm sure he does."

"Well all right then. I'm going to give Winston some tuna now." She takes the cat into her flat and closes the door.

Greg looks at me and lets out a sigh. "Well at least that's sorted."

I nod. "Until next time."

Kishawn pulls on my sleeve and looks up at me. "I think Jordan took something. That's why he won't open his hands."

"No, I didn't!" Jordan says.

I look at him and see that his hands are still closed into fists. "Have you got something, Jordan?"

He shakes his head but doesn't open his hands.

"He's always taking things," Kishawn says. "Mum says he's a klepto-something."

"No, I'm not!" Jordan says, taking off towards the stairs.

We all follow him but he's so fast, we don't catch up to him until he's on the second floor, outside our flat. There's nowhere else for him to run so he's standing with his arms folded tightly.

I crouch in front of him. "What have you got, Jordan?"

"Nothing," he whines, shaking head.

I hold out my hand. "Whatever it is, it doesn't belong to you. You should give it to me and I'll return it to its rightful owner."

"No, he'll be mad at me for taking it."

"Who will?"

"The man downstairs. The man who doesn't like cats."

"I'm sure he won't be mad if we explain to him that you took it by accident. And if you apologise. You know that taking things is wrong, don't you?"

He nods hesitantly.

"It's because he's a klepto-shaman-ack," Kishawn offers.

"Why don't you give me what you took?" I say to Jordan.

He holds out his fist and opens it. A single item drops from his fingers and I catch it.

When I open my hand and see what he took from Rob's flat, my breath catches in my throat.

Lying on my palm is a scrunched up red ribbon.

## CHAPTER 19

It is Saturday night and it is cold. The sky is clear of clouds, the stars and moon shining down on him brightly as he parks the Land Rover on the North Terrace, the road that runs along the top of Whitby's West Cliff. Most of the buildings here are hotels and B&Bs. All of their windows are dark.

The parking meters are covered with canvas hoods that bear a sign saying, *Parking Free Until 1st of March*. There are no other people around.

He walk north from the car and finds the tarmac path that angles down the cliff to the beach below. The tide is coming in but there is still a sliver of sand visible in the moonlight.

He descends the steep path as quickly as he dares, eager to get to the ice cold water but also wary of slipping and falling to the cement promenade below.

When he reaches the promenade, he descends the concrete steps to the beach and then pauses to take in his surroundings. The area seems deserted, the town slumbering. The only sound is the rhythmic rush of the waves as they sweep over the sand.

Satisfied that he is alone, he removes his clothes and strides across the sand towards the waiting sea. The cold night air pricks his skin but he knows this is nothing compared to what he will feel once he is in the frigid water.

As he reaches the sea's edge and the waves lap over his ankles, he gasps with exhilaration. The water is so cold it numbs his feet almost immediately.

He wades deeper into the surf, hearing its roar louder now, feeling it creep up his legs like tendrils of questing ice. When the water reaches his chest, it takes his breath away. He forces himself to breathe slowly and deeply, filling his lungs with salty sea air.

A wave lifts his feet off the sand and pushes him towards shore. He fights it, cutting through the water with his arms to swim out deeper.

After a couple of minutes swimming, he pauses, treads water, and looks back at the beach. He's gone out a long way, despite the tide trying to wash him back to shore. His feet can't touch the bottom anymore.

He takes a deep breath, then lets it out slowly, sinking beneath the surface as he does so. He keeps his eyes closed as he sinks, letting the sensation of being pulled into the cold depths trigger a memory he has cherished for seventeen years.

As the cold envelops him completely, he lets his mind drift back through time, remembering the moment he was suspended in water so cold he felt as if it had frozen his heart into a shard of ice.

That was when he saw her.

He opens his eyes now and sees nothing but darkness. But in his mind's eye, he remembers the woman floating before him, her blonde hair shimmering around her head like a halo, her unseeing blue eyes staring at him, the red ribbon twisting and turning in that halo of bright hair.

His lungs scream for oxygen. His chest tightens painfully. Part of him wonders if it might be better to just let the memory take him, to sink into its alluring pull forever.

But another, stronger part of him desires to make the memory flesh again. To transform this echo of a point in time into something real that he can gaze upon and love.

He struggles to the surface and gulps in air, feeling the pain in his lungs diminish to a dull ache. This isn't his time to die. He has work to do. Another storm is coming soon and he needs to prepare.

Relaxing his body, he lets the tide wash him ashore as if he is a piece of driftwood. When he finally clambers out of the water, muscles as useless as blocks of ice, he collapses on the sand and stares up at the moon and the stars. They stare down at him like bright eyes.

He longs for storm clouds to fill the sky and hide him from their sight.

## CHAPTER 20

The ribbon sits on the coffee table between me and Greg. It's Sunday evening and Jordan and Kishawn have gone home, collected by Nia and Will a few hours ago. I don't know how their weekend getaway went other than a wink Nia gave me when they arrived at the flat. I'm sure she'll tell me more when we get a chance to talk.

We didn't mention the ribbon incident. It's become a sore point between me and Greg. He thinks the fact that Rob North had a red ribbon in his flat means nothing whereas I think it means everything.

The ribbon has been sitting on the coffee table for almost 24 hours now, the subject of discussions and arguments so heated that they belie the pedestrian nature of the object.

"Are we going to throw the silly thing away now?" Greg asks.

"No, we're not. It might be evidence."

He sighs. "Evidence of what exactly?"

I shrug. I don't need to spell it out for him. He knows what I think.

"Kate, you're not thinking about this rationally."

I shoot him a look that says, *Don't even go there.*

He falls quiet for a couple of seconds and when he speaks again, his tone is of someone trying to seek reason. "Rob doesn't have the physicality for what you're thinking. Can you really imagine him carrying dead bodies over the moors and burying them?"

"You have no clue about any of this, do you? The women were drowned and then just left where they died. He didn't have to carry them anywhere and he certainly didn't bury anyone." *Except possibly Caroline Shields*, I add mentally to myself. *He might have buried Caroline.*

"So how exactly did he lure these women to remote places to kill them? He's hardly Ryan Gosling."

"I don't know. But I do know that the women are always found with a red ribbon in their hair. And the first woman to go missing lived in this flat. If you can't see the connections, Greg, then you need your eyes examining."

"The woman who lived in this flat was never found, with or without a red ribbon. So your leap of logic doesn't really make sense. And then making a further leap that because Rob has a red ribbon he must be a serial killer is a stretch even for you."

"What is that supposed to mean?"

He folds his arms and turns his face towards the window. "Nothing."

"No, come on, I want to hear what you've got to say. A leap of logic and a stretch of the imagination. Elaborate."

"You know what I'm going to say."

"I want to hear you say it."

He takes in a deep breath and lets it out slowly before speaking again. "You were wrong about Simon Coates. Look at the trouble that caused. If he'd sued us, we could have lost everything."

"So I was wrong for trying to help a woman discover the truth about her son's death?"

"That isn't what you were doing and you know

it. You've lived your whole life unable to face the fact that sometimes people die for no good reason. There isn't always a killer lurking in the shadows. You can't face the fact that Max died accidentally so when Stella Coates came to you saying she suspected her husband, you jumped at the chance to help her. You saw yourself in Stella, didn't you? Well, you're both alike, I'll give you that; neither of you can face reality."

Hot, stinging tears blur my vision. I don't even know why I'm crying. Part of it is anger but a larger part of it is the feeling of betrayal. I thought Greg was on my side. I thought he knew that I was only trying to help Stella. She was so distraught, so lost, so alone.

I can't be here, in this flat, right now. I need to get out, to get some air. Snatching up my car keys, I head for the door.

"Kate, where are you going?"

"Out. I need some time to think."

He gets up, comes over to me, puts a hand on my shoulder. "No, come on, there's no need for this. I didn't mean—"

"Don't touch me, Greg." Shrugging his hand away, I march out into the hallway and down the stairs. When I get outside, the cold evening air dries my tears and makes me shiver. I should have brought my coat but I'm not going back for it now.

I blast the heat up in the Mini and drive out onto the road, unsure of which direction to take. The road that leads north across the moors looks uninviting so I instead turn south towards town.

As I begin my journey, a couple of flakes of snow appear in the headlights. The entire country is supposed to be getting snow and high winds this coming week so these few innocent-looking flakes might herald something much worse.

I turn on the wipers and listen to their intermittent *whirr* as I drive.

When I reach Whitby, I follow the signs for the West Cliff and park by one of the covered parking meters. Despite the fact that I don't have my coat, I get out of the car and wander to the edge the cliff, careful not to get too close.

The lights of fishing boats shine in the distance, looking like lone stars that have broken away from the constellation of lights that shine from the houses and streets. High up on the East Cliff, across the river from where I stand, the abbey is a dark shadow against the night sky, a battle-worn sentinel watching over the town.

The waves below the cliff wash over the sand in

an unceasing advance as the tide comes in and a full moon hangs behind the snow-filled clouds, brightening their edges with a crisp, silver luminescence.

Wet flakes of snow drift down onto my face and melt into tiny pools of icy water that run down my cheeks, leaving a trail of cold sharpness on my skin.

I experience a clarity of thought, as if I've been dragged into wakefulness from a long, deep dream. No one is going to help me prove what I believe to be true: that Rob North is involved in Caroline Shields' disappearance and might also be connected to the murders of the women on the moors. Not Greg. Not the police. Not anyone.

Because of the mistake I made in the past, I'm what's known as an unreliable witness. No one will take what I say on face value, not even my own husband. Before anyone is going to listen to me, I need irrefutable proof.

A plan formulates in my mind and by the time I return to the Mini, I'm cold and wet but I have direction.

I'm going to find the truth, no matter what.

## CHAPTER 21

When Ivy opens her door on Monday morning, she looks weary until she sees my face and smiles. "Hello, dear. Come for a cuppa?"

"That would be nice." I follow her into the kitchen but instead of taking my usual seat at the table, I hover near the drawers. "Why don't I help you?"

"Oh, there's no need for that, dear. I've been making tea since before you were born."

"Still, it's nice to have a hand every now and then." I open the cutlery drawer and take out a spoon, pulling the drawer out more than necessary and leaning down slightly so I can see if what I want is hiding behind the plastic cutlery organiser. Yes, there's a bunch of keys sitting there.

I close the drawer and give Ivy the spoon.

"Thank you, dear." She's arranging the cups and saucers while she waits for the kettle to boil.

"Where's Winston today?" I ask, looking around the flat for the cat. He'd be rubbing around my legs by now if he were here.

"Oh, he's gone out. I told him it was going to snow again today but he cried and cried at the door so I told him to do his business and then come straight home." She looks at a clock on the wall and a tinge of worry enters her voice. "But that was over an hour ago."

"Do you want me to go and look for him?"

"Would you, dear? That would be very kind. I'll have the tea waiting for you when you get back."

"All right." I go outside and call Winston, hugging myself against the chill. Like Ivy said, the forecast is for snow later today but for now at least, the dark clouds above are only threatening to cover the world with white. Last night's few flakes didn't amount to much and the snow on the ground this morning is barely more than a light powder.

There's no sign of the cat. I go around the back of the house and call him again, wishing I'd brought a tin of tuna out here to entice him back from wherever he's lurking.

I set off down the garden, looking to see if Winston is hiding in the bushes, when I notice that the shed door is slightly ajar. I can also see bootprints in the powdering of snow on the grass, leading from the house to the shed.

I hesitate. If Rob's in there, I don't want to go down there. On the other hand, what if Winston is in the shed with him? I did tell Ivy I'd get her cat back and after Rob's implied threat the other day, I'm not sure I'd trust him in a shed with Winston.

Steeling myself, I march down to the bottom of the garden and open the shed door fully.

There's someone in there, rummaging around in a pile of gardening tools. It isn't Rob; the person's frame isn't big enough. When he stands up and turns to face me, I see that it's Mike.

There's a shelf that runs along the wall of the shed, holding tins of paint and weatherproof treatment for fences. Winston is strolling along the shelf, tail in the air, purring loudly.

"Kate," Mike says. "What are you doing here?"

"Sorry, I was just looking for Winston. Ivy's a bit worried about him."

He reaches out to the cat and rubs his ears.

"Yeah, he followed me in here. I'm just looking for some duct tape. One of my kitchen cupboards is coming off its hinges."

"Do you have a key then?" I point at the open padlock hanging from the door.

"Oh, yeah. The key is kept under the plant pot just outside the door. Don't tell Rob I told you that." He smiles conspiratorially. "I often come in here for supplies if I need to fix something in my flat. No point waiting for that tosser to get around to it."

"You really don't like him, do you?"

He seems unsure how to answer that. Then he shrugs. "Do you?"

I shake my head. "No, not really." Then I casually add, "Do you know how he got those scars? Ivy said he was in some sort of accident."

Mike nods. "Car accident."

"Ivy thinks it...affected him."

"Yeah, well who wouldn't be affected by something like that? It's a good job Mummy and Daddy gave him a place to live and a job to do because otherwise, I think he'd be out on the streets."

He searches through the shelves and finds what he's looking for. "Aha, here we are! Just what I need." He picks up a roll of grey duct tape.

"I'd best take Winston inside," I say, taking the cat into my arms. He's heavy but at least he doesn't fight me. Instead, he purrs and rubs his face under my chin.

"Sure thing. See you later."

I take Winston out of the shed and retrace my steps up the garden towards the house, thinking it strange that I didn't see Mike leave the house while I was in Ivy's flat. He'd have to walk past her open door to get out to the garden.

As I get closer to the house, I realise why I didn't see Mike come out here; his bootprints that lead down the lawn to the shed don't originate at Northmoor House's main door. They come from the back door.

I stop on the path and examine the tracks. They're the only prints in the snow so they're definitely Mike's. Does he have a key to the back door as well as the shed?

That doesn't make sense. Mike's flat is on the first floor so why would he have a key to an entrance door on the ground floor?

He comes out of the shed and closes the

padlock before squirrelling the key away under a plant pot.

Before he sees me loitering at the back door, I quickly go around the corner and in through the main entrance.

Ivy is sitting at her kitchen table, the teapot and cups arranged before her. When she sees Winston, her face lights up. "Winston, I told you not to go out there today. You're a very naughty boy."

I put the cat down and he goes over to Ivy, winding around the legs of her chair.

"Thank you for finding him, dear. I expect he was in the bushes."

"No," I say, taking the seat across from her. "He was in the shed with Mike."

"Oh, he's a lovely young man. He always strokes Winston when he sees him."

"Do you know much about him? Mike, I mean."

She pours the tea and ponders. "Well, not much, really. I think he works in York. Very pleasant chap."

While we drink our tea, I keep an eye on Ivy's open door to see it Mike will come walking past. When he doesn't, I assume he must have entered the house the same way he left it, via the back door. But how can he get from the back door up to his flat? There aren't any steps up to the first floor other than the main staircase.

"Are you all right, dear?" Ivy asks and I realise I've zoned out.

"Yes, I'm fine," I say, offering her a smile.

She starts to tell me about Winston's favourite hiding spots outside and I nod and smile at the right places but my mind is elsewhere. I'm contemplating the possibility of Northmoor House having secret staircases and hidden rooms. Maybe I've just read too many Gothic Romance books.

But a secret staircase would explain how I heard footsteps in the attic, even though the hatch was closed and locked.

It makes my mission to get the keys from Ivy's drawer even more imperative.

I stir my tea and purposely drop the spoon onto the floor. It's a move that wouldn't fool anyone but Ivy is looking down at Winston and rubbing him between the ears so she doesn't suspect anything.

"Oh," I say, "I'll get another spoon."

Ivy pushes her chair back. "Let me get it, dear."

"No, no, you stay there." I spring from my chair

and pull open the cutlery drawer, blocking Ivy's view with my body as I reach into the pile of spoons in the organiser and jangle them together to hide the noise of the keys as I pick them up and push them into my pocket. They bulge against my jeans and I feel they're so obvious that Ivy is bound to notice them.

Quickly retaking my seat, I stir my tea noisily, chinking the spoon against the china cup to draw Ivy's attention there and away from my face, which I'm sure looks guilty. I feel bad about taking the keys but she doesn't use them and I need them for something important.

If I'm going to have a good look around Rob's flat, I need to get in there somehow.

# CHAPTER 22

Dani stands beside her Land Rover Discovery at the side of the moor. Above the sprawling landscape, dark clouds roll across the January sky and a light fall of snow has begun. The winter breeze blows the flakes into her face and over the Land Rover. She ignores the snow. Wrapped up in a padded winter jacket and black knit watch cap, she barely feels the cold. Her attention is on the expanse of moorland in front of her.

The Land Rover's passenger door opens and DS Matt Flowers climbs out. Similarly attired to Dani, in padded winter clothing, he shouldn't feel the cold either but he rubs his hands together as if to warm them. "We've been here half an hour, Guv."

Without taking her eyes off the moors, Dani nods slightly. "And we might be here for another half an hour."

He follows her gaze across the wintry landscape. "I don't understand what we're doing here."

"I told you on the way. This is where Caroline Shields' car was found."

"I know that but what are we looking for?"

"We're not looking for anything in particular, Matt. I'm thinking."

He looks up at the darkening sky. "This snow is going to get worse fairly soon."

Dani nods. "Just like the night the car was found in the ditch. Heavy snow, freezing temperatures. So why would she drive along this road?"

"She was on her way to a Christmas party, if I remember correctly."

"The party was in Scarborough. She should have been driving south on the A171, not heading north through the moors."

"You have a theory don't you, Guv?" They've worked together long enough that he knows when Dani is putting a scenario together in her head.

"I don't think Caroline was ever here at all. I

think someone dumped the car here to make it look like she went off the road that night and wandered away from her vehicle into the storm."

He nods. "That was the prevailing theory at the time, Guv. That she slid off the road and got lost in the snowstorm."

"It doesn't make sense. The car is in the wrong place and Caroline wasn't dressed appropriately. Her neighbour said she was going to the Christmas party dressed as Snow White. Can you honestly see someone wandering over the moors in a snowstorm dressed as a Disney princess?"

"No, Guv."

"No. If she'd had an accident and ended up in the ditch, she'd have stayed with the car and phoned for help."

Matt considers this and nods. "Okay but if Caroline wasn't driving the car, then who was?"

"The person who killed her."

"Killed her? It's a missing persons case, Guv."

"Yeah, but maybe it should be more than that. I want to show you something." She leads him back to the Land Rover and gets into the driver's seat while he clambers in the passenger side.

Picking up the Caroline Shields case file from the back seat, Dani opens it to the page that contains an inventory of items found in Caroline's flat on the night she disappeared.

"Look at the inventory," she tells Matt. "There was no hair dye found in the bathroom and no packets that might have contained hair dye in the bins in the flat or the wheelie bins outside."

He frowns. "Hair dye?"

Bringing up a picture of Snow White on her phone, she shows it to him. "Snow White has black hair. Caroline didn't bother dying her hair black, which means she was dressed up as Snow White but with her usual blonde hair."

Matt shrugs. "A blonde Snow White. I'm not following, Guv."

She taps her finger against the picture on the phone. "What does Snow White have in her hair?"

Realisation dawns on him and his eyes widen. "A red ribbon. You think our man did this?"

"It fits the trigger theory Maya Cho told me about," Dani says. "The killer saw Caroline Shields wearing a red ribbon and that started him off on his killing series."

Matt looks out of the window at the snow. "So he's killed five women just because he saw someone dressed up as Snow White?"

Dani nods. "Apparently. The question is: where

is Caroline's body? He didn't leave her on the moors like the others."

"Maybe he buried her."

She's already considered that possibility. "How could he? The ground was frozen."

Matt thinks about that for a moment and then shrugs.

"I think he killed her somewhere else and then drove her car up here so the police would look in the wrong place," Dani tells him. "Henson's team spent all their time combing the moors but they should have been searching elsewhere."

"But where?"

"Probably the last place Caroline was seen alive. Northmoor House."

"You think she was killed at home?"

"Wouldn't it make sense? The last person to see her alive was her neighbour Ivy Rose. Caroline went down to Ivy's flat to show off her costume. That was the last anyone saw of her. In Ivy's statement, she says she heard Caroline drive away half an hour later but she didn't actually look out of the window and see her. What she heard could have been the killer driving away in Caroline's car."

"I suppose that makes sense. But surely Henson's team analysed Caroline's flat."

"Henson was quite thorough, actually," Dani tells him. "He processed Caroline's flat meticulously. There were no signs of a struggle and no blood. But, of course, there wouldn't be either of those things if it was our man, would there? He drugs them first and then drowns them."

Matt nods slowly. He seems to be running the possibilities over in his head.

"And it explains the car's location," Dani continues. "The killer knew Caroline was going out to a fancy dress party but he didn't know it was in Scarborough. So instead of dumping the car on the A171 and making it look like Caroline disappeared on the way to the party, he put the car in the wrong place."

"It makes sense, Guv."

"There's a map in the glove box. Let's have a look at it."

Matt fishes the map out and opens it. It's an Ordnance Survey Explorer map of the North Yorkshire Moors. At a scale of 1:25,000, it shows the area in great detail, including buildings and walking trails.

"Right, this is where we are now," Dani says,

pointing her gloved finger at the road on which they're currently parked. She traces her finger east along the map until she finds the building marked *Northmoor House*. "And this is where he probably killed Caroline. So he drives out onto this road, leaves the car here and then walks back to Northmoor House. I'd say that looks like maybe three miles. It wouldn't be too much of a problem for someone who is fit and determined to walk three miles in a snowstorm."

Matt is frowning at the map.

"What's wrong?"

"Why go back to Northmoor House at all? Why wouldn't he flee the area?" Sudden understanding crosses his face. "Of course! He had to go back to Northmoor House to collect the body, put it into his own vehicle, and drive away with it."

"That isn't the assumption I'm working on," she says.

He looks crestfallen. "So what do you think, Guv?"

"First of all, we're saying Caroline was the trigger, that he saw her wearing the ribbon and that kicked off his paraphilia, right?"

"If paraphilia means his compulsion to kill, then yeah."

"So he couldn't have just been some passerby who happened to see Caroline through her window, could he? She lived on the top floor of the house."

"So to see her in the Snow White costume, he had to have been inside the house that evening," Matt suggests.

"Exactly. That's why I don't think the killer returned to the house just to collect Caroline's body. I think he returned to Northmoor House because he lives there."

## CHAPTER 23

I have to wait two days before I finally hear Rob go out in his Land Rover. I know he's reclusive and the thick snow on the ground is enough to deter anyone from going out but I've spent the last couple of days driven to distraction by my impatience. I've also been fretting in case Ivy discovers the keys are gone from her kitchen drawer.

But now the green Land Rover has finally rumbled out of the parking area and headed off towards town. This is my chance.

I grab the keys from where I've been hiding them, in the bottom drawer of my bedside table, and go downstairs quickly. If Ivy's door is open, I'm not going to be able to enter Rob's flat because she'll see me. And even though she most likely wouldn't tell Rob and would be all for me sneaking in there, I don't want to make her complicit in my actions. What I'm about to do is illegal and Ivy is better off knowing nothing about it.

I breathe a sigh of relief when I get to the ground floor; Ivy's door is closed.

Wasting no time, I stop in front of Rob's door and select a key from the key ring. There are nine keys on the ring and I have no idea which one fits Rob's door. It isn't the first one I try, or the second, but when I insert my third choice, the lock clicks open.

Trying to be as quiet as I can, I go through the door and close it gently behind me. Rob has left his lights on so I don't have any trouble descending the short flight of steps to the second door, which is already open, revealing the little basement flat beyond.

The place really smells unpleasant but I ignore that and cross the room to the bedroom door. It's in here that Rob has his computer and desk and that's where I've decided I'm going to start first.

The women on the walls watch me as I go to the desk and try the top drawer. It opens. Inside, there's a haphazard collection of wires and computer parts and a few balled up tissues. I don't touch any of it and quickly move down the next drawer.

In here, there are more wires, fighting for drawer space with CDs of games and a couple of pairs of headphones. Closing the drawer, I feel frustration building inside me. I have to remain calm and methodical. It isn't like I was going to find a signed confession in here or anything like that but Rob's general untidiness made me think he'd be careless enough to leave something incriminating just lying around on display.

Now that I'm down here looking around, it's obvious that he's more careful than I'd thought.

Crouching down, I pull the bottom drawer open, expecting to see more bloody wires, and am surprised to find a black nylon zippered pouch. It feels so light when I take it out of the drawer that for a moment I think it's empty. But when I unzip it, it opens to reveal a number of plastic inserts, each holding a memory card. The cards aren't labelled in any way so there is no way of knowing what they contain. They might even be empty.

I can't take the pouch if I want to keep my break-in a secret but maybe I can take one or two memory cards and they won't be missed. I leaf through the plastic inserts and remove two cards from the rearmost page. Rob won't notice they've gone unless he leafs through the inserts himself. I zip the pouch back up and close the drawer.

Standing up, I put the two cards into my pocket and wonder if I should look in the bedside table or the wardrobe next. Deciding to try the bedside table, I open the bottom drawer first this time.

Sitting in the drawer is a Disney pencil case. I pick it up and examine it. It's pink and has pictures of the Disney princesses on its sides. It feels like there are a couple of pens and pencils inside. I open it and look at them. This is Caroline Shields' pencil case and these are her things. Caroline was right in thinking Rob had stolen them from the flat.

So that confirms Rob is a thief but not that he's a murderer. I close the drawer and check the top drawer which contains men's magazines and various medications ranging from over the counter painkillers and cold remedies to another box of Valium that matches the one sitting on top of the bedside table.

There's no collection of red ribbons, no trophies from the murdered women—unless you count Caroline's pencil case—and nothing to link

Rob to the murders on the moors. This is disheartening. I didn't expect to find concrete evidence that proves Rob is the Red Ribbon Killer but I expected to find *something*, even if it's just a tiny lead.

Unless the memory cards in my pocket reveal something useful, my illegal entry of Rob's flat has been pointless.

The wardrobe is my only hope now but as I move towards it, I hear Rob's Land Rover outside. Damn, I thought he'd be away for longer than this. Everything in the bedroom seems to be put back correctly so I leave the room and cross the living room to the door. I hear Rob slam his car door outside.

Rushing up the stairs, I pull the bunch of keys from my pocket. I can't remember which one I used to get in here. I should have made a mark on it.

I get out into the hallway and close the door. Rob's silhouette is visible though the frosted glass of the main entrance door, getting larger as he approaches the house. Leaving his door unlocked, I run for the stairs.

As I turn the corner and vault up the first two steps, I barrel into Mike. He falls backwards and drops the black bin bag he was carrying. "Whoa! Steady there!"

I stumble as I try to keep my balance but end up landing on my backside next to him. "Sorry. I didn't see you."

Rob is in the hallway now, going towards his front door.

Maybe he'll think he forgot to lock up when he left.

Mike gets to his feet and picks up the black bag. He smiles at me. "I didn't realise taking my rubbish to the wheelie bin could be so dangerous."

I clamber to my feet. "I'm so sorry, Mike. Are you okay?"

"I'm fine. How about you?"

"Yeah, I'm okay."

He holds the bag aloft. "Good job I wasn't carrying anything breakable."

I hear Rob's door open. He's realised now that it wasn't locked. Will he think he forgot to lock it or will he suspect something? There's no way he hasn't heard me and Mike on the stairs. Will he suspect us?

Mike finishes his descent of the steps and I begin the climb up to my floor. I hear Rob say to Mike, "Hey, have you been in my flat?"

"Don't be ridiculous," Mike replies.

I hear him go outside to the wheelie bins and then I continue up to my flat.

Once inside, I lean against the door and let out a long sigh of relief. Rob might suspect that someone has been in his flat but he can't prove anything. And the next time he goes out, I'm going to put the memory cards back where I found them. He'll never know I was there.

But for now, I want to look at what's on them.

There's a card reader in my desk drawer. Fishing it out of there, I plug it into the computer and push one of the cards into it. A new folder appears on the computer screen, containing the data held on the card.

I open it.

# CHAPTER 24

"No, I won't authorise an investigation into Northmoor House," Superintendent Brian Holloway says, throwing Dani's report down onto his desk. "All you have here is supposition and fantasy."

Dani groans inwardly. Even while she was writing the report to request that she and her team be given permission to investigate the tenants of Northmoor House—and possibly even get a warrant to search the place—she knew it was a long shot. Holloway likes to act on certainties, not suppositions, and she'll be the first to admit that her theory is no more than supposition and seemed tenuous at best when she put it down on paper two days ago to hand in to the Super.

But that's why she needs to look into it more deeply; to confirm her suspicions.

After not hearing a word from Holloway for two days regarding her report, she'd hoped he was considering its merits. But now that hope is dashed against the boulders of bureaucracy and Holloway's pig-headedness.

"It isn't even your investigation," he says, obviously determined to expand upon his reasons for rejecting her request. "Jack Henson did a damn fine job with the Caroline Shields case and you're saying he made mistakes."

So it came down to this, did it? The old boys' club? Holloway always had Henson's back because they were both products of the same private school in Cambridge and shared stories about teachers there. "No, sir, I'm not saying that. DI Henson didn't have the knowledge we have now regarding the Snow Killer. He was working in the dark because Caroline went missing before the Snow Killer came to light. I'm just saying that with hindsight—"

"So what am I supposed to tell the press? Hmm? That we thought this serial killer was beating us 4-0 but now we're revising it to 5-0 because one of our Detective Inspectors has a hunch?"

"It isn't a hunch, sir. It's a logical deduction."

"Logical deduction? You're not Sherlock Holmes, Summers."

"And this isn't a football game, sir. If he's killed five women, then that's what we should report. We're talking about people's lives. There isn't a scorecard."

"There is in the papers. This so-called Snow Killer is making us look like fools. Perhaps if you spent more time on that case—the case you've been assigned to—instead of meddling in an old missing persons case, we'd be closer to catching the bastard."

"If you read my report, sir, you'll see how I believe the Snow Killer case may be related to the events surrounding Caroline Shields' disappearance."

"Yes, yes, I've read the report. Cars in the wrong place, Snow White wandering over the moors, bodies that can't be buried in the frozen ground. It's all very entertaining but there isn't a single shred of evidence to support any of it. Do you have something to back up these theories? Something concrete?"

"No, sir, that's why I need to investigate further."

He leans across the desk towards her. "What you need to investigate, Detective Inspector Summers, is the multiple murder case to which you have been assigned. If that case isn't holding your interest, perhaps you'd prefer to be taken off it and assigned to something else."

Dani's heart sinks. She's been working the Snow Killer case for so long now and has put so much work and time into it that she has to be there when the bastard is finally caught. "No, sir, I'd like to remain on my current case."

He slides her report across the desk towards her. "Good, then we'll have no more of this nonsense. Is that understood?"

She swallows her pride and nods. "Yes, sir."

He sits back in his chair and puts his hands together, steepling his fingers beneath his chin. "That will be all, Detective Summers."

She gets up and leaves his office. It's a short walk along the corridor to the room where her team are working hard on the Snow Killer case. As she enters, Matt Flowers looks up from his desk and raises his eyebrows questioningly.

Dani shakes her head and rolls her eyes, a

gesture she's used many times after coming out of Holloway's office.

She drops into her chair and wonders what her next move is going to be regarding the case. Despite what Holloway thinks, the Northmoor House theory was worth a closer look. But now she's basically been told to stay away or lose the Snow Killer case.

Matt comes over to her desk. "No joy, Guv?"

"That's putting it mildly."

"That bad?"

"Let's just say we won't be pursuing any lines of inquiry regarding Northmoor House or the disappearance of Caroline Shields."

He slams his fist into his palm. "Bloody red tape!"

"Holloway is in charge, Matt. We have to respect that."

He looks repentant of his outburst, embarrassed even. "Of course, Guv."

She empathises with him and would be swearing about it herself if not for her position. She has to keep morale high, despite everyone's frustration at the length of time this case has gone on for with no real leads or suspects.

"Instead of commiserating about the stuff we

can't investigate," she tells Matt, "lets work our arses off on the stuff we can and catch this bastard."

Matt gives her an enthusiastic nod. "Yes, Guv."

Dani opens the Amy Donovan file and reads the forensic and post-mortem reports again. As she does so, her attention constantly wanders to the Caroline Shields case file that sits on her desk apart from those of the Snow Killer's victims. Dani is sure Caroline belongs with Stephanie, Nicola, Angela, and Amy but unless some sort of concrete evidence emerges to prove it, Caroline will remain separate from the other women.

Dani silently vows that if Caroline belongs with these other women, she will bring her into the fold somehow. She won't let Caroline's fate remain a mystery simply because Holloway is too afraid of how he'll be perceived in the press.

She reaches for Caroline's file and places it beneath the pile of the Snow Killer's victims.

With Henson's departure, the department seems to have forgotten Caroline.

Dani won't.

## CHAPTER 25

The files inside the memory card's folder are titled with dates and strings of numbers of the type automatically assigned by a computer. I open one that is dated October, two years ago, and a photograph of Caroline Shields appears on the screen. Dressed in a green parka and jeans, she's walking across the parking area towards the entrance door of Northmoor House with shopping bags in her hands. The picture seems to have been taken from the rear corner of the house. It was certainly taken without Caroline's knowledge.

I close the file and click on an earlier one dated July 12 of the same year. This one is a video. It shows Caroline leaving her flat—this flat—and walking along the corridor towards the stairs. She's wearing a sun top and a light floral skirt and she has sunglasses pushed up on top of her hair, which is tied back into a ponytail. The image is black and white and was obviously captured by the security camera near the lift.

After Caroline passes beneath the camera, the file ends, making me think this brief section was edited from a larger video or was recorded live and the recording was stopped when Caroline passed from view.

Scanning through the thumbnails of the other files in the folder, I see that they're all photos and videos of Caroline going about her life, unaware that she's being recorded and photographed.

So at the very least, Rob was stalking her. Did that escalate into something more?

Removing the card from the reader and inserting the second card reveals more of the same. Hundreds of photos and videos of Caroline.

But as I scroll through the thumbnails, one of the videos catches my eye. Unlike the others, which are all recorded from the camera at the end of the hallway, this one seems to show Caroline inside the flat.

I click on it and it opens to show Caroline watching telly. It seems to be evening time and she's wearing a pink dressing gown with white hearts on it. Her hair looks wet, as if she's been in the shower. The view is from outside the living room window and the video runs for ten minutes before ending.

I swivel in my chair to face the window. I checked for cameras before because I didn't understand how Rob seemed to know Greg was going into the attic before we even left the flat. But I didn't think to check outside the window.

Crossing the living room, I keep my eyes trained on the black plastic flower box out there, searching for a lens. I can't see anything. When I reach the sash window, I slide it open, letting the freezing wind and snow into the flat.

Crouching closer to the window box, I see a tiny camera pointing into the flat. It's no bigger than a button and there's no way I'd see it if I wasn't looking for it.

But it's seen me. And it saw Caroline in the months before she went missing. Rob was down there in the basement flat watching and recording. Has he recorded me as well? Are there photos of me on a memory card in that nylon pouch in his desk?

Taking the camera between my thumb and forefinger, I try to pull it away from the flower box but it seems to be glued to the plastic so I go into the kitchen and get a knife. Sliding the knife between the flower box and the camera, I manage to pry it loose.

Then I take it between my fingers again and pull. It rips away from the plastic and I inspect it. There are no wires. It probably works on Wi-Fi and is filming me even now.

Disgusted at the thought, I drop it beneath my foot and stamp on it with my heel. It cracks but I don't know if it's still working or not so I stamp on it again. And again. Until it's nothing more than a broken disc of plastic and glass on the floor.

I want to go downstairs, hammer on Rob's door and confront him. I want to throw the broken camera in his face and follow that up with a tirade of abuse and maybe a couple of punches.

But I know I can't do that.

I have to go to the police, show them the camera and the images of Caroline on the memory cards. If nothing else, at least he'll be arrested on a stalking charge.

*And I'll be arrested for burglary. The police will want to know how I got my hands on the images and videos of Caroline. Rob could press charges.*

*I could be facing prison time.*

I close the window, shutting out the wind and the snow, and pace the flat, the broken camera in my hand. I need to draw the attention of the police onto Rob but somehow keep from mentioning the images of Caroline on the memory cards I stole.

While I'm thinking, I hear a car door slam in the parking area and hear Rob's Land Rover start up. He's going out again. This is my chance to return the cards.

Peering out of the window, I watch him pull out of his parking space and drive away. There's no time to waste. Before I return the cards, I save the folders from both of them onto my hard drive. Just in case. Then I go downstairs.

My heart sinks when I get to the ground floor and see that Ivy's door is open and Winston is wandering around in the hallway. During my descent of the stairs, I've formulated a plan that is sure to bring the police here with a search warrant. I can't have Ivy telling them that she saw the nice lady from the top floor going into Rob's flat while he was out.

I wonder if I can slip in through Rob's door unseen but as I'm wondering that, Ivy appears in the hallway. "Oh, hello, dear. Would you like a cuppa?"

"I would, thank you," I say, fixing a smile onto my face. "I need to go out to my car first, though, so maybe you should take Winston into your flat and close the door. We wouldn't want him going out on a day like today, would we?"

"He won't follow you out if you close the door behind you, dear. Rob left a minute ago and Winston didn't follow him outside. Good job, too; that waste of space would probably lob another snowball at him." She turns and goes back into her flat. "Now I'll get the kettle on so don't be too long."

I watch her shuffle into her kitchen and wonder how quickly I can get to Rob's desk drawer and back out again. Ivy tends to stand at the kitchen counter with her back to the door while she waits for the kettle to boil so maybe I can get in and out without her knowing what I'm up to.

Telling myself not to overthink it and just do it, I go to Rob's door and start inserting keys into the lock, looking for the right one. Winston winds around my legs, purring. I have to make sure the cat doesn't go through the door with me.

When the lock finally clicks open, I reach down and pick Winston up, gently tossing him away from the door before opening it and slipping inside. This time, I keep the correct key pressed between my thumb and forefinger so I can lock the door quickly when I leave. I won't make that mistake again.

I stride into the bedroom and open the bottom drawer. The pouch seems to be exactly how I left it so Rob probably doesn't even know two of the cards were missing. I replace them and zip the pouch up before striding back across the room, up the steps, and out into the hallway. Winston is waiting for me and trots over to me with his tail aloft.

Ivy is pouring water from the kettle into the teapot. Remembering her super-hearing, I realise she'll know if I haven't actually been outside so I go out the door and wander over to my car. There's something I need to do before I have tea with Ivy anyway.

I open my car and slide into the driver's seat, taking my phone out of my pocket as I do so.

The plan I formulated on the stairs goes into action as I dial Jillian Street's number. She doesn't answer but I get her voicemail.

I wait for the beep and then say, "Jillian, it's Kate Lumley. Call me back when you get this. I've got a story for you."

## CHAPTER 26

The bar of the Marine Hotel is tidy and pleasant, with a dozen or so patrons eating seafood and chatting. The mouth-watering smell of kippers, smoked haddock, and lobsters in garlic is making my stomach rumble but I'm too nervous to eat. On the table in front of me is a glass of white wine to calm my nerves.

Jillian called me back ten minutes after I left the message on her voicemail and suggested we meet here. After a hurried cup of tea with Ivy, I donned my winter gear and drove to town, parking by the railway station in my usual spot.

My jacket, hat, and gloves are on the seat next to me. It's warm in here and the atmosphere is soporific. If this were any other day, I'd probably sink a little deeper into the seat and enjoy my wine while watching the world go by outside the window.

But not today. Today, my mind is whirling, wondering if my plan will work. I've recited the exact words I'm going to say to Jillian over and over in my head. There must be no room for error. She can't misinterpret anything I say. The story must be printed exactly as I tell it.

Knowing Jillian, she'll try to put a spin on my words, make the story more sensational. I can't open up any areas of conversation where she might mine a nugget she can use for her own ends. I have to be careful because she'll probably know I'm not telling her everything and she'll try to dig deeper to find what I'm hiding.

I see her through the window, walking by the railing that skirts the harbour, wearing a long coat and boots. She seems oblivious to the cold, facing the wind with no hat or gloves. Her long blonde hair blows across her face and she absently brushes it away from her eyes before kicking snow off her boots and entering the bar.

She sees me straight away and waves, going over to the bar and making a drinking motion at me with raised, questioning eyebrows. I lift my wine glass to show her it's still half full and she gives me a thumbs up before ordering her own drink.

When she comes over to the table, she's holding a glass of red. She sets it down on the table in front of her and takes a seat opposite me. "Nice to see you again, Kate. You said you had a story for me?" Taking her phone out of her handbag, she places it next to her wineglass. "Do you mind if I record our conversation?"

I shake my head. "No, that's fine."

She finds the voice recorder on her phone and presses the record button before placing the phone between us on the table. Then she takes a sip of wine and nods appreciatively before putting the glass back down. "So, what have you got for me?"

"Have you ever heard the name Caroline Shields?"

"Caroline Shields. Isn't she the girl that went missing a couple of years ago?"

I nod. "That's right. No one knows what happened to her."

"Okay," she says, leaning forward slightly. "Tell me more."

I reach into the pocket of my jacket and take out the crushed camera. I show it to Jillian and put it down next to her phone. "That's a spy camera. The landlord at the flats where I live has been spying on me."

She frowns. "You've gone off on a bit of a tangent there, Kate. How does this relate to Caroline Shields?"

"I'm getting to that. The landlord's name is Robert North. I assume that before I moved into the flat, he spied on the previous tenant as well. Probably recorded her day to day activities."

Jillian nods slowly, obviously not seeing where this is leading but biding her time like a spider patiently waiting for an unwary insect to fly into its web.

"The previous tenant was Caroline Shields," I tell her.

Her eyes widen. "So this guy, this Robert North, was watching the missing girl before she went missing. Do you think he—"

"No," I lie, unwilling to go down that route. "I just think he might have evidence, maybe even something he doesn't know he has. If he recorded Caroline on the day she disappeared, there might be something on the recording that the police could use to find out what happened to her."

She sits back in her seat, thinking quietly for a

moment before saying, "Why are you giving this to me? It has all the elements of a front page story. A missing girl being secretly filmed by a pervert. That's the kind of thing the public loves."

"I don't have any contacts in the industry anymore." This is true but it isn't the reason I want Jillian to have the story. The fact is, I don't want anything to do with the world I used to inhabit, the world that chewed me up and spat me out. I never want to be a butterfly on that wheel again.

After taking another sip of wine, Jillian studies me closely. The easy air of camaraderie with which she greeted me outside the antiques shop the other day is gone. In its place grows a seed of suspicion. "There's something you're not telling me," she concludes.

There's plenty I'm not telling her: the fact that I suspect Rob has something to do with Caroline's disappearance; my logical reasoning that, by extension, he could also be the Red Ribbon Killer; and my certainty that the police have made an error in not questioning him two years ago.

I can't tell Jillian any of those things. She has to think that this is simply about Caroline and a possible recording the police don't know about. If she gets even an inkling that this story may be connected to the Red Ribbon Killer, she'll go diving into that angle and probably investigate it for months before she's ready to sell a story to the highest bidder.

She has to think this is nothing more than the story of a pervy stalker who may have caught more on his spy camera than he realises. That way, she'll sell the story fairly soon. Once it appears in the papers, the police will have to act.

DI Summers has obviously ignored what I told her at the Captain's Table, or doesn't think it warrants further investigation so I'm going to force her hand. She won't be able to ignore a media outcry. She'll have to take Rob in for questioning and search his flat.

And then she'll find the images on the memory cards in his desk and whatever else might be on his computer.

"There's nothing else," I tell Jillian, putting on my best poker face. "Except that I want my name kept out of it."

She scrutinises me for a moment and then sighs resignedly. "Okay, what's the address of these flats?"

"Northmoor House."

"I'll need to take this," she says, reaching for the broken spy camera.

"No." I grab her hand. "You can take a photo of it but I'm hanging on to it."

She sighs again, as if I'm being unreasonable. "Fine, I'll take some pics of it." She uses her phone to photograph it on the table and I put the camera back into my jacket pocket.

Jillian downs her wine and gets up from the table. "I'll have to send my photographer around to the flats to see if he can get a shot of this Robert North fellow looking furtive. What does he look like?"

"He's a big guy with a scar on his head. He usually wears a baseball cap."

"Scar huh? How'd he get that"

"A car accident when he was younger, I think."

"Right, I'll look into that as well. Thanks for this, Kate. It isn't much of a story on the face of it but if it turns out that he has a video that helps in the case of Caroline Shields' disappearance, some good will be done by publishing it."

I give her a brief smile. Her motivation is nowhere as altruistic as she's trying to make it sound and we both know it. What she really wants is to be known as the crime reporter who found evidence the police were unaware of. If that evidence solves the case, then all the better. Not for Caroline's family but for her. She's probably already mentally planning a book and talk show tour.

If that means she's going to push to get the story published as soon as possible, all the better. It might even save a life. If Rob is the Red Ribbon Killer, he isn't going to be able to murder another woman while the attention of the media and the police is trained on him.

Jillian leaves the bar walks back the way she came, along the harbour. Certain that I've done the right thing by giving her the story, I finish my wine put my jacket and hat on before going out onto the street and ambling back to my car.

The snow has finally stopped falling and although there's a thick covering of it everywhere, the sun has begun to peek out from behind the clouds.

When I get into the Mini, I sit behind the wheel for a moment, feeling a surge of emotions welling up inside me. Once the story is published, Greg and I are going to have to move again. I can't accuse the landlord of being a peeping tom and expect to remain in the flat. I haven't even mentioned any of this to Greg. And now I've made an irrevocable decision regarding our future.

I had no choice. I did it for Caroline, to make sure her case is looked at properly by the police. If that means sacrificing our tenancy at the flat, then so be it. We can always move somewhere else but Caroline will only have one chance for justice.

Telling myself again that I've done the right thing, I start the engine and pull out of the car park.

O———⚷

He watches from the shadows of the railway station building as Kate drives out of the car park. He's been watching her for a while now, his attention caught by her blonde hair, high cheekbones, and blue eyes.

The weather report says that freezing temperatures are on their way in a couple of days. He can wait until then. He *has* to wait until then because the conditions must be just right before he can carry out his work.

Everything has to be perfect.

The snowfall must be perfect. The temperature must be perfect. The girl must be perfect.

Of all the girls he has considered, Kate looks the most perfect. She looks the most like his original, beloved sleeping angel.

When he ties a red ribbon into her hair and watches it splay out around her face as she lies in cold water, it will almost be as if his sweet Astrid has come back to him.

Especially when Kate's unseeing eyes stare up at him through a layer of ice.

CHAPTER 27

"What the hell is this, Summers?" Superintendent
Holloway asks as he slams the newspaper down
onto his desk. "Is this something to do with you?"

Dani, sitting opposite him, glances at the
headline which reads PERVY LANDLORD MAY
KNOW WHEREABOUTS OF MISSING GIRL and
sighs. It isn't the most lurid headline she's read
about Rob North today but it's still bad enough to
make her wince inwardly. "Sir, you know I would
never speak to the press about anything like this."

"Really? You might see why I find that hard to
believe. You came into this very office a couple of
days ago telling me you wanted to question this
Rob North chap and now this appears in the
paper. Are you trying to force my hand?"

"No, sir, but I think someone is."

"Who?"

"The woman I met in the Captain's Table. She pointed out to me that Rob North wasn't questioned in the initial inquiry. She's obviously told one of her reporter friends the same thing."

"Only now there's a rumour that a camera might have been recording what went on in Caroline Shields' flat. How the hell was that missed at the time?"

"I don't know, sir. As you pointed out, it wasn't my case."

His face darkens and he points his finger at her. "Don't get sassy with me, Summers."

Dani says nothing. The story makes the police look incompetent but if she plays this right, she could turn it to her advantage. The spy camera stuff might amount to nothing but at least it will open a back door for her to investigate the Caroline Shields case. That's if Holloway doesn't assign it to another detective out of spite.

"Anyway," he says, "the unnamed woman who reckons she found a spy camera in her flat hasn't come to the police about it. Unless she presses charges, we're not obliged to do anything."

"Even if there's a chance the landlord might

have some evidence regarding the Caroline Shields case? What if he's responsible for her disappearance? Can you imagine the media frenzy if we ignore this and it turns out to have some truth behind it?"

Holloway looks worried and Dani knows he's thinking about how he's going to look to the press. There's already a group of journalists outside headquarters and she's willing to bet there are even more at Northmoor House, trying to get Robert North to say a few words.

"Well what do you suggest?" Holloway says.

"Let me and DS Flowers go round there with a couple of uniforms to pick him up. The uniforms can bring him back to the station while DS Flowers and I execute a search warrant on his flat. We'll bring back his computer for forensic analysis and any other electronic devices which may contain images or video of Caroline Shields.

"If it comes to nothing and he's just a peeping tom, then at least we'll have been seen to have done something. If we find images relating to Caroline, they could help us build that case closer to a conclusion. It's win-win, sir."

He mulls that over, nodding slowly. "Yes, I can't see a downside. All right, Summers, get it sorted and bring this peeping landlord in. I want him in a custody suite by the end of the day."

"Yes, sir," she says, getting out of her chair. "Shall we use Scarborough? It's closest to Whitby." The building in which they are situated, the North Yorkshire Police Headquarters in Northallerton, has no custody suite. The closest cells are located at Harrogate Police Station. She doesn't fancy driving almost two hours from Northmoor House to Harrogate when Scarborough Police Station is only forty minutes down the road.

"You sort out the logistics, Summers. Just make sure something good comes out of this one way or another. We can't have stories like this floating about." He brandishes the newspaper before throwing it into the bin next to his desk.

"I'm on it, sir." Dani leaves the office and closes the door behind her before she goes in search of Matt.

CHAPTER 28

I'm awoken by a commotion outside Northmoor House. A quick glance through the window lets me know Jillian Street's story has been published. The road outside the house is full of vehicles and there's a throng of journalists at the main door, some of them banging on it and shouting, "Mister North, are you in there? Would you like to give us your side of the story?" It seems that Rob has locked the door.

There's a text on my phone from Greg that reads: *A couple of news vans were arriving at the house this morning. Wonder what that's about.*

Once Jillian's story broke, it wouldn't have taken long for the journalists to make their way over here since most of them were already in town covering the Amy Donovan story anyway. Luckily, Greg left for work before the main herd arrived.

That means I don't have to explain anything to Greg just yet. In the cold light of day, with the house under siege from the press, I'm beginning to regret talking to Jillian. This is exactly the same thing I had to endure after my story appeared in the Manchester Recorder. I'd felt afraid and alone, as if I were being hunted by a pack of wolves.

Now, I've brought that ravenous wolf pack to someone else's door.

*He deserves it. He spied on you and he spied on Caroline and he's probably done something much worse than that.*

I try to mentally justify my actions but at the moment, with the banging and shouts drifting up from below, it's difficult. Still, this is the only way to get the police here; they can't ignore the possibility of new evidence in the Caroline Shields case.

Sitting at my desk, I switch the computer on and check the news. I want to see exactly what Jillian Street published. The headline of the day's top story shouts at me from the screen.

DOES THIS PEEPING TOM KNOW WHAT HAPPENED TO MISSING GIRL?

Beneath the headline, there's a photo of Rob

"looking furtive" as Jillian would put it. He's actually just unaware that he's being photographed and is glancing across the parking area as he walks away from his Land Rover.

It's a totally innocent glance but Jillian's photographer—who must have been hiding in the back garden—has captured a microsecond of expression which makes it look like Rob is looking into the camera with narrowed, suspicious eyes before he embarks upon some sort of clandestine activity.

The article, which thankfully doesn't mention my name but describes me as a "worried tenant living in fear," explicitly states that Rob has been recording the activities of everyone in the flats at Northmoor House. Jillian is taking a gamble with that statement, especially since she knows nothing about any recordings, but I can see why she's done it; without recordings, the story amounts to nothing.

She then states that "missing girl Caroline Shields" lived in the top floor flat when she vanished and that "the perverted landlord, who has been scarred since childhood after a car accident in Norway and has been shunned by society because of his disfigurement" has recordings of her life, possibly even of "her final moments" that the police will want to see.

Even knowing Jillian's tendency for hyperbole, the suggestion that Rob has been "shunned by society because of his "disfigurement" is a bit much. If Rob has been shunned by anyone, then surely that's because of his personality, not the scar on his head.

One thing that interests me in the article is the fact that the car accident happened in Norway. My curiosity is piqued so I conduct a search on the Net. Using the terms *Norway*, *car accident*, *Fred North*, and *Wanda North*, reveals only one result in English. The others appear to be in Norwegian. Obviously the accident wasn't considered newsworthy here and is only mentioned in local reports.

The link takes me to a news article that is published in English as well as Norwegian entitled TWO FEARED DEAD AFTER ACCIDENT AT LAKE. The article is dated December 13th, 2002. There is no photo, and only two blocks of text.


Two people are feared dead after a collision at Lake Femund yesterday. In the late evening, during heavy snowfall, a hired Volvo, driven by Fred North from the United Kingdom as he was returning to his hotel with his family, collided with a Volkswagen driven by Astrid Andersen, 23, from the village of Elgå.

Both cars crashed through the ice and into the lake. Three members of the North family were taken to hospital. Miss Andersen and the North family's eldest son are believed to be dead. A search for their bodies will begin when the weather clears. The cause of the collision is believed to be ice on the roads coupled with reduced visibility due to heavy snowfall.

Closing the page, I sit back in the chair, feeling a sudden flood of empathy for Rob North. How old would he have been in 2002? Probably eight or nine, possibly ten years old. And he lost his brother on holiday. Just like I did. Like me, he probably feels that he needs someone to blame for his brother's death, that an accidental verdict is too cruel.

Maybe he blames Astrid Andersen, the woman

who was behind the wheel of the other car. Does that rage build up inside him all year until it's finally released in winter, when the snow reminds him of the accident?

It sounds plausible to me but I'm no psychologist.

A sudden blast of a police siren brings me to the window. A police car is pulling into the parking area, lights flashing, with a dark green Land Rover Discovery close behind. The sirens seemed to be a warning to the journalists, who scatter as the vehicles roll up to the door of the house.

Two uniformed officers get out of the patrol car and DI Summer gets out of the Land Rover along with a man I guess to be another detective. They go to the door and one of the uniformed officers knocks loudly. "Robert North, this is the police. Let us in."

I leave the flat and go downstairs. If Rob isn't going to let the police in, then I will. We can't have them knocking the door down.

When I get downstairs, Ivy has beaten me to it. She's shuffling to the door and saying, "Just a second." She reaches up and releases the Yale lock.

The police come inside. "He's in there," Ivy says, pointing at Rob's door.

While a uniformed officer knocks on Rob's door, DI Summers comes over to me. "I want a word with you."

I nod. "We'd best go up to my flat."

"Take care of things down here, Matt," she tells her plainclothes colleague before following me upstairs.

"Would you like a cup of tea or anything?" I ask her as we enter the flat.

"No, thank you. I'm going to need the spy camera you found in your flat, though."

I take the camera out of my jacket pocket and had it over. She holds it out on her palm, frowning at it. "Was it in this condition when you found it?"

"No, I did that. I was angry at having my privacy invaded."

She nods understandingly. "And you went to the papers instead of the police because..." She leaves her words dangling in the air between us.

"Because I told you about Rob North not being questioned regarding Caroline and you didn't do anything about it."

Holding up the spy camera, she asks, "So did

you really find this in your flat or is it a ruse to get us here? Because if that's the case—"

"It's nothing like that. I found the camera attached to the window box. He really has been spying on the flat."

"Do you have any proof that he was doing so when Caroline lived here?"

I shake my head. There's no need to tell her about the memory cards; the police will find them when they search Rob's flat.

But there is one more thing I think she should see. I pick the red ribbon up off the coffee table and hand it to her. "This is from his flat. I was looking after my friend's children and one of them went into the basement flat. He came out with this in his hand."

She turns it over in her hand. "Has anyone else touched this?"

"Jordan, me, my husband, probably Jordan's sister."

She rolls her eyes and turns towards the door. "Right, I'll see if I can get to the bottom of all this." She pauses at the door and turns back to face me. "I don't know whether to be mad at you or thank you."

"Maybe you shouldn't do either just yet," I tell her.

She nods. "I'll be in touch." She goes out into the hallway and closes the door.

I can't just sit here on my own while all of this is going on. I follow the detective downstairs and get to the ground floor hallway just in time to see Rob being taken out of the main entrance door by the uniformed police. He looks lost and frightened. As soon as the door opens, there's a flurry of activity outside. Questions are thrown at Rob and cameras flash bright.

DI Summers puts on a pair of latex gloves and goes into Rob's flat. I go to Ivy's and find her sitting on her sofa, petting Winston who is curled up in her lap.

"Hello, Ivy," I say from the door. "Are you all right?"

She looks at me but her face doesn't brighten as usual. There's a worried look in her eyes and her mouth is set into a straight line.

"Do you want me to make you a cup of tea?" I ask, going into the flat.

She nods slowly. "Yes, that would be nice. Thank you, dear."

"Is anything the matter?" I crouch down so that we're at eye level.

"It's just all these police and reporters. It reminds me of when we had all that trouble before. When the girl upstairs vanished."

"Caroline," I say.

"Yes, Caroline. She was such a pretty thing. Always full of life, you know? And then one day she was gone. Just like that."

"The police will probably get it all sorted out," I assure her. "That's why they're here."

Outside, there's another blast of the siren as the patrol car tries to get past the horde of reporters and cameramen.

"See, they're taking Rob for questioning," I tell Ivy.

She tightens her lips and frowns as if trying to remember something. "But he wasn't here."

"I know and that's why they're questioning him now, because they didn't do it before. Now, you just relax and I'll make you a nice cuppa." I go into the kitchen and put the kettle on. Just as it comes to the boil, all of the electrics go off. The kitchen is plunged into shadows and there's a sudden silence as the low hum of the fridge dies.

"Bloody hell." I pour the hot water into the

teapot then go into the living room where there's at least some light coming in through the windows. "That's just what we need," I say to Ivy.

Instead of her usual rant, she nods absently.

"Ivy, are you sure you're all right?"

DI Summers and her colleague walk past the open door with Rob's computer and a number of cardboard boxes in their hands. I go to the window and watch them load everything into the back of the Discovery. The journalists crowd around them, asking questions and trying to photograph everything.

Ivy hasn't answered me. She's staring at the dead TV, a look of confusion on her face. "This isn't right," she mutters. "He wasn't here. He wasn't here."

"Who wasn't here, Ivy?"

"Rob. He wasn't here."

"Yes, I know. Rob wasn't here when the police came around. You told me that before. Don't worry, it's all going to be sorted out."

She shakes her head. "He wasn't here that night either. The night she was dressed up like Snow White. This isn't right. They shouldn't be taking him away."

Her confusion must be contagious because

now I don't know what she's talking about. "You told me Rob wasn't here when the police came around asking questions about Caroline. You told them he was dodgy and offered to let them into his flat. Remember?"

"Yes, I remember that. And he is dodgy. Never fixing things when he's supposed to. Going out at all hours and doing God-knows-what. Not to mention throwing snowballs at cats. But he didn't do anything to Caroline. He'd never do anything like that. He couldn't."

"Ivy, listen to me," I say, crouching down to her level and taking her cool hand in mine. "Rob has been filming the upstairs flat. He had a camera in the window box recording everything. He took photos of Caroline without her knowing."

"Yes, he's a creep," she says. "I know that. We all know that. But he isn't anything more than that. He hasn't got the get-up-and-go to be anything more than that has he? He's too bloody lazy."

"Well, the police will get to the bottom of it." I pat her hand and go back into the kitchen to pour the tea.

As I'm arranging the cups, I hear Ivy mutter to herself. "He wasn't even here."

## CHAPTER 29

Dani sits impatiently in the interview room at Scarborough police station next to Matt Flowers. She looks at the two empty seats on the other side of the table and taps her pen on her notebook. Robert North has been conferring with the duty solicitor in a private room for almost an hour now.

She turns to Matt. "What's taking so bloody long?"

"Got to get his story straight, Guv."

"He can't talk his way out of this, no matter how he spins it." On the table in front of her are a number of pictures printed from memory cards found in Robert North's desk drawer. They show Caroline Shields in her flat, in the hallway of Northmoor House, and in the parking area. The computer they took from the flat is in the cybercrime unit, waiting to be forensically analysed. Unfortunately it's in a queue but Dani has enough to go on with the memory card pictures. For now anyway.

"Do you think he's our man, Guv?"

She's asked herself this question a hundred times already today. Is Robert North the Snow Killer? The evidence they've found so far certainly makes him a suspect but when Dani looks at the man, she finds it hard to believe he's the killer they've been tracking for the past two years. Still, she isn't going to dismiss him that easily.

The door opens and North enters the room, followed by the duty solicitor. They both take their seats at the table.

"You do the honours," Dani tells Matt.

He starts the recorder and states the date, time, and who is in the room.

"Now then, Mr North, we have a few questions for you," Dani says, "What can you tell me about—"

"Before we begin," the duty solicitor says, "I have a written statement signed by Robert North that he would like me to read out and then give to you."

"Go ahead," Dani says, sitting back in her chair. *Here comes the story he's spent the past hour formulating.*

The duty solicitor produces a piece of paper and reads from it. "*I, Robert Daniel North, admit that I set up a camera that pointed into the top floor flat at Northmoor House. I did so for security reasons and did not intend to invade anyone's privacy.*

*Furthermore, I would like to point out that I was out of the country when Caroline Shields, the resident in the top floor flat, went missing. I was in Benidorm, Spain visiting my parents from the 12th of December to the 4th of January.*"

Dani feels herself stiffen but doesn't let her face betray any emotion. Why the hell wasn't this in the case file? The report she read simply said that Robert North wasn't at home when the constables visited Northmoor House nor was he interviewed at a later date. The report didn't say that was because he was on bloody holiday.

The duty solicitor slides the statement across the table towards Dani. She leaves it there, checks the clock on the wall and says, "Interview paused at 11:23 a.m."

Two minutes later, in the corridor outside the

interview room, she says to Matt, "Find out if that's true about him being in Spain."

"Yes, Guv." He takes out his phone and begins dialling.

Dani pushes through a number of doors until she's outside the station, standing on the snowy pavement as the traffic rumbles past on Northway. She can't believe that someone in Henson's team made a cock up like this. How is she supposed to catch a killer when the inquiry reports aren't filled in correctly?

Matt comes outside and offers her a sheepish smile. "I was just talking to one of the constables who did the interviews at Northmoor House. He told me that the reason they didn't go back to interview Robert North was because they found out he was in Benidorm visiting his parents. They confirmed it at the time. There's no doubt about it; he was in Spain."

"So why wasn't it in the report?"

He shrugs helplessly. "I don't know, Guv."

She begins to pace the pavement, frustration building. *What else did Henson's team miss? What else isn't in the report?*

"Come on,"she says to Matt as she goes back into the police station. "We're going to go through the case file with a fine-tooth comb. There's something we're not seeing."

"Regarding Robert North?"

She shakes her head exasperatedly. "No, not him. We've got him on a voyeurism charge but he wasn't in the country when Caroline went missing or when Stephanie Wilmot was murdered."

"So what are you thinking, Guv?"

She leads him through the corridors to the room they were using before the interview, unlocks it, and ushers him inside. The Caroline Shields case file sits on one of the desks next to a computer that is currently switched off.

"Take a seat," Dani says to Matt, gesturing to one of the chairs. She goes to a whiteboard on the wall that has a number of figures written on it and wipes them off with her hand. From a holder attached to the board, she removes a blue marker and writes:

*Snow White*

*Diazepam*

*Red Ribbon*

"Should I take notes?" Matt asks.

"No, I'll do the writing. We need to brainstorm these three things to start with." Pointing to the words *Red Ribbon*, she says, "Why did Robert North have a red ribbon in his flat? We know he isn't the Snow Killer so is this red ribbon just a coincidence?"

"That's a hell of a coincidence, Guv."

"Agreed. And then there's the diazepam. Robert North just happens to have a considerable quantity of the same drug the killer uses to sedate his victims. Another coincidence?"

Matt shrugs. "I don't know. Maybe he just has trouble sleeping. He had a lot of painkillers in his bedside table as well. It probably relates to the accident he was in when he was a child."

"The accident," Dani says, writing the word on the right side of the board. She draws a line connecting the word *Accident* with the word *Diazepam*. "Get on to Sandra and see if she can find out more about this accident. Tell her to contact the Norwegian police if she has to."

Matt calls DC Sandra Sharp at Headquarters while Dani studies the words on the board. The words *Snow White* leap out at her. She turns to Matt, who is still on the phone. "Didn't we find a Disney pencil case in Robert North's flat?"

He purses his lips for a moment and then nods.

She writes *Pencil Case* on the board and draws a line between it and *Snow White*.

Matt ends the call. "She's been on to the Norwegian police already and they're sending her some information, apparently."

"Great. What we know so far is that Robert North's brother was killed in the accident along with a young Norwegian woman, right?"

"That's all we could find in English."

She writes *Brother* and *Norwegian Woman* beneath the word *Accident*.

"I think her name was Astrid, Guv."

"What?"

"The Norwegian woman. Her name was Astrid." He consults his notes. "Astrid Andersen."

Dani erases the words *Norwegian Woman* and writes the name in their place. "What about North's brother? What was his name?"

"No idea," Matt says. "We only know Astrid's name because it was mentioned in the Norwegian news article."

"We need to find out the brother's name."

Matt looks doubtful. "Are you sure we should be spending our time on this, Guv? The accident happened nearly twenty year ago."

"I want all the information I can get. Now, this Disney pencil case we found in North's flat. Do you think it's his?"

"Doesn't fit in with the other stuff he owns."

"No, it doesn't. But it does fit in with the items found in Caroline Shields' flat. She was a big Disney fan. That's why she was dressed up as Snow White for the Christmas party."

"Maybe North stole the pencil case from her flat. He's the landlord so he'd definitely have a key."

"And the red ribbon?"

"He probably stole that from Caroline as well."

Dani writes the words *Snow Killer* at the top of the board and circles them. She draws lines from the circle to connect it to the words *Diazepam* and *Red Ribbon*. "You can see the problem, Matt; the same drug the killer uses and a red ribbon were found in the possession of a man who lives in the same building as Caroline Shields. This is more than a coincidence."

"But Robert North was in Spain."

She nods. "He was in Spain so he had nothing to do with Caroline's disappearance." She draws a question mark on the board and connects it to the words *Snow Killer*. Jabbing at it with the marker, she says, "So who is this? He has access to the same drugs and he saw Caroline that night in her Snow White costume."

Matt's phone rings. He answers it. "What have you got for me?" He listens for a couple of minutes then turns on the computer at the desk and logs into the network. "Yeah, mail those over to me, Sandra. Thanks."

He ends the call and looks at Dani. "The Norwegian police are going to phone Sandra with more details about the accident but for now, they've sent her some photos that were taken at the scene. She says there are two that we really need to see. She's sending them over."

Dani leans on the back of Matt's chair while he opens his email. There's a message from Sandra with two image attachments, entitled AstridAndersen1 and AstridAndersen2. Matt double clicks the first one and it opens up to show the shoreline of a lake. A snow-covered beach sweeps down to the water where sheets of ice float on the surface. In the shallows, Dani can see a human shape floating beneath the ice. She can't see any details because the photo was taken from some distance away—to establish the location, she guesses—and captures the scene rather than the details of the person under the ice. The only thing Dani can see clearly is the dark green parka the corpse is wearing.

"Try the next one," she tells Matt. He clicks the image and it fills the screen.

Dani's breath catches. Although this photo was taken almost twenty years ago, the image it shows perfectly matches four images that are burned into Dani's brain.

Astrid Andersen is lying on her back beneath the ice, her eyes staring up at the sky. She looks tranquil in death, a serene beauty perfectly displayed like a butterfly under glass. Her blonde hair floats around her head like a halo and floating within that halo is a single red ribbon.

## CHAPTER 30

After having tea with Ivy, I go back up to my own flat and peer out of the window. The journalists have finally gone, probably driven away by the weather. The snow is coming down so heavily and so fast that I can't see anything at all beyond the parking area.

Sitting on the sofa, I glance over at a silver-framed photograph of Greg that was taken on our wedding day. He's smartly dressed in a morning coat, smiling at the camera like he doesn't have a care in the world. A pang of guilt brings hot tears to my eyes. I should have told him that I was going to the papers with my story. Part of me knows that the reason I didn't is because he would have tried to talk me out of it.

Picking up my phone, I decide to ring him at work. It wouldn't be right for him to hear about all of this from the news. Of course, I might be too late; he's probably already seen a newspaper headline or heard about it on the radio. What must he be thinking?

The phone tells me there's no service and I throw it back onto the coffee table. Bloody power cut. That means I can't work either. Not that I'd be able to anyway; my mind keeps replaying the events of this morning and I'm constantly wondering what's going on at the police station where they're holding Rob. Have they uncovered some piece of evidence that links him to Caroline's death and possibly those of the other women?

While I'm sitting there in the gloom, I hear a noise from the kitchen like a slow ticking. When I realise what it is, I push myself up from the sofa and storm in there. The leak is back. Water has pooled on the ceiling and it slowly dripping into the sink. I have an urge to go out into the hallway and break open the padlock on the attic hatch. Rob isn't here to stop me.

But then I realise I don't need to break into the attic. I have a set of keys that probably fit all the locks in the house. Not the padlock, of course, since that was put there recently and the keys I have are old. But they will fit the house's back door, which has to be the secret way into the attic. I know there isn't a brick wall behind that door because I know Mike used the door to go to and from the shed. And I know there's another way into the attic because I heard footsteps up there when the hatch was closed and locked.

And since there aren't any other doors that could possibly lead up there, the back door is the only possible explanation. There must be a secret stairway that leads up to the top of the house.

At least if I see where the leak is coming through the roof, I can put a bucket underneath it. Grabbing my phone in case I need to use its light to see by, I put on my coat and hat and take the bunch of keys out of my bedside table drawer.

Northmoor House is dark and silent as I go downstairs. Ivy's door is closed and Rob's has a length of blue and white police tape stretched across it. Outside, the snow has formed a thick layer on the ground. It shrouds my Mini, Mike's Volvo, and Rob's Land Rover.

I walk past the cars and around to the back of the house, blinking away the cold snowflakes that land in my eyes. When I get to the black door, I select the largest key, a long iron thing that looks like it's about a hundred years old, and place it into the lock. When I turn it, the lock clicks open.

Wasting no time out here in the snow, I open the door and slip inside.

I'm in a small, square room whose walls are of bare brick. Against one wall stands a metal ladder. I go to its foot and stare up into darkness. I can't see how high it goes but I'm guessing it reaches all the way to the attic.

I turn on the Flashlight app on my phone and direct the light up along the ladder. It barely reaches a few feet before the dark swallows it.

Determined to find the leak, I put one foot on the bottom rung and give the ladder an experimental shake. It feels sturdy enough. Still I hesitate. I'm not really afraid of heights but climbing up into the darkness is unnerving.

Stepping up onto the ladder, I realise that I'm not only going up into the attic to find the source of the leak but also to see what else is up there. Rob looked panicked when Greg was going to go up and have a look so I'm sure there's more hidden up there than just junk.

Climbing the ladder while holding the phone up to light my way proves difficult. It means I can only use one hand to hold onto the metal rungs and every time I let go to grab a higher rung, I have to wrap the arm holding the phone around the ladder to hold myself steady. This isn't going to work.

I stuff the phone into my jeans and I'm suddenly plunged into complete blackness. At least I can use both hands on the ladder, though. I take it easy, making sure my feet are firmly planted on the rung below me before reaching up for the one above. In this manner, I make slow progress but after a couple of minutes, I'm sure I must be approaching the attic.

Stopping to check, I take the phone out of my pocket and turn on the light. Just a few more feet to a square opening above. I put the phone back into my pocket and climb the remaining rungs.

When I'm through the open hatch, I use the phone to check my surroundings.

I'm in the attic. The beam of light reveals wooden beams and the slant of the roof above my head. The floor is wooden, fashioned of rough floorboards. I step off the ladder and the boards creak beneath my weight.

Even though the phone's light doesn't reach far and I can't see the far end of the attic, I can tell that the room I'm in is expansive. A quick inspection of the roof above me doesn't reveal any holes. In fact, the roof looks like it's in good repair. Still, I need to find the area that is situated above our kitchen. There must be a hole or missing tile there.

Trying to mentally gauge the distance and direction of our kitchen from where I'm standing now, I walk forward a few steps before something on the wall catches my eye. Stepping closer, I see that there are two newspaper clippings taped to the bricks. Beneath the clippings is a small table bearing various items.

The newspaper articles are old and yellowed by age. Only the headlines are readable, the smaller type having faded into illegibility over the years.

The first headline says, *Car Crash Kills Young Boy*.

The second piece of newspaper once had a small photo beneath the headline but it's now nothing more than a light grey square. The words above the square of faded ink read, *Scandinavian Police Search For Missing Woman And Boy*.

On the table beneath the pieces of paper sits a framed photo. It shows a young Fred and Wanda North standing by a red Volvo with two young boys. It's snowing and everyone is swaddled up in winter gear. I'd put the older boy at twelve or thirteen. The younger looks eight-years-old, the same age Max was when he died. Although I know the younger boy is Rob, I don't recognise him because both boys have scarves wrapped around their faces. This was obviously taken on the Scandinavian holiday, before the accident.

Why is the photo up here in the attic? Is this some sort of shrine Rob has built to his dead older brother? Is this where he comes to mourn?

Replacing the framed picture on the table, I walk in the direction I believe our kitchen is located, checking the roof as I go. It all seems waterproof so far.

Then I see a bulky object ahead of me, a darkness within the shadows. Expecting it to be a piece of furniture, I aim the light at it. The beam illuminates a large chest freezer. It's plugged into a socket on the wall but at the moment, it isn't running because of the power cut.

When I see a hole in the side of the metal, near the freezer's base, I realise that the leak we've been experiencing in our flat isn't due to a faulty roof at all. The power cuts are causing the ice in the freezer to melt and it's leaking out onto the floorboards before finding its way down to our flat.

Someone has put grey duct tape over the hole but it hasn't done much good; the water is flowing freely onto the floorboards.

I'm not sure why Rob would keep a freezer in the attic, although having seen the size of the basement flat I suppose it makes sense. There's no room for a freezer down there, especially one as big as this.

"What does he keep in here?" I ask myself. "A thousand frozen pizzas?"

I open the lid and look into the freezer. Inside is a solid block of ice that reaches all the way up to the lip, as if the freezer was filled with water at one time and then left to freeze. If Rob has food in here, there's no way he can get to it. The ice is covered with a coating of frost.

Curious as to why anyone would run a freezer with nothing but ice inside, I wipe the frost away with my hand.

When I see a face in the ice, I stumble backwards, dropping the phone. It slides across the floorboards and ends up face down, the light shining straight up at the roof beams above.

I grab it with trembling hands and get up,

turning back to the freezer. My heart hammers in my chest and my blood pumps so forcefully, I can feel it in my ears and head. I can't have seen what I thought I saw. I just can't.

Peering into the freezer again, I see the face in the ice. Although I never met her in life, I know it's Caroline Shields. She's wearing a Snow White outfit and there's a red ribbon in her hair.

Somewhere within me, a well of emotion overflows and I start to cry. I feel like I knew Caroline. We lived in the same space, looked out of the same window at the same view. Like me, she spent time having cups of tea with Ivy and Winston.

I was certain she was dead all along but having it confirmed like this, finding her inside a freezer above our kitchen, is too terrible for words. With hot tears stinging my eyes, I close the lid and make my way back across the attic to the ladder.

I have to tell the police. I can't ring them because there's no signal in the house. I have to drive to town. They need to know about Caroline's body.

At least they already have Rob in custody.

I descend the ladder as fast as I dare in the dark and push out through the back door into the garden, blinking as daylight hits my eyes. I lock the door. The attic is a crime scene now. As well as that, I feel a need to keep Caroline secure. I know that doesn't make sense since she's probably been up there for two years already but now that I know she's there, I won't leave the door unlocked.

My car keys are in my jacket pocket. I fish them out and walk through the falling snow to the Mini. I quickly brush the snow off the windscreen and get in. The car starts immediately and I put the wipers on to clear the rear window but they're frozen solid and don't work.

Anxious to get moving, I dial the heating up to full blast and get out. I quickly wipe the snow off the rear window and climb back in behind the wheel. There's still a layer of ice on both windscreens and on the windows but I can't wait around. I press the accelerator and the car lurches forward. As I drive onto the road, something doesn't feel right; the steering feels loose, as if I have a flat tyre. I can't have a flat, though; the onboard computer would tell me if one of the tyres were flat or even had reduced air pressure.

Putting the car's handling problems down to the snow and ice under the tyres, I pull onto the road that leads to town and maintain a steady speed. The first part of the journey involves driving along the road that cuts through part of the moors. It doesn't look like any other cars have been this way for a while—the road ahead is white and smooth with virgin snow—but the roads closer to town should be well-travelled and clearer.

The moors on the left side of the road are lost behind a curtain of thick snow. To the right, the cliffs and the sea are barely visible. The ice on the windscreen is finally beginning to melt but the falling snow is obscuring my vision, streaking down the glass in wet rivulets. Without the use of the windscreen wipers, I can't go much farther before I'm going to have to stop and wipe it away.

A sudden bang from the back of the car surprises me. The Mini feels like its tipping to the left and now there's a horrendous scraping sound. I jam on the brakes and the car slews towards the edge of the road. Releasing the brake and trying to regain control, I turn the wheel to the left—into the skid as I've read or heard somewhere—but it's too late. The Mini slides into the ditch with a jolt that slams me forwards against my seatbelt.

I take the belt off and get out, stumbling up the side of the snowy ditch and onto the road. I don't understand what happened. Did I get a puncture?

An inspection of the car reveals something that shocks me; the rear left wheel is missing. It isn't just punctured; it isn't there at all. I turn and look back along the road and see the wheel lying there, a black circle against the white snow.

How the hell did the wheel fall off? It isn't possible.

*Unless someone loosened or removed the wheel bolts.*

Did Rob do this? After he saw the story about him, did he go out to the parking area and loosen my tyre?

I check my phone. Still no service.

I'm stuck. The Mini is stuck in the ditch and I can't put the tyre back on without the bolts.

I also can't stay here forever because I'll freeze to death.

So I either go back to the car and sit inside with the heating on, hoping someone will drive past, or I walk back to Northmoor House.

As I'm debating on which course of action to take, I hear an engine rumbling in the distance. I can't see the vehicle because of the falling snow but it definitely sounds like it's getting closer.

When I finally see the dark shape coming

through the snow, I step out into the middle of the road to flag it down.

As it gets closer, I realise that I know this vehicle; it's Rob's dark green Land Rover.

For a crazy moment, I wonder if the police have released him for some reason, if he saw me leave the house and followed me.

No, that's not possible. It can't be Rob. He's at the police station. This can't be him.

The Land Rover slows down and comes to a dead stop. The windscreen is covered by a thin layer of ice and that, combined with the snow falling into my eyes, obscures the driver.

My mind races. What if it is Rob? What will I do?

I'll run onto the moors. I can outrun Rob. I might even be able to double back here and take the Land Rover.

The driver climbs out of the car. My muscles tense as I prepare to flee.

"You need some help?" he asks.

I let out a long sigh of relief.

It isn't Rob.

It's Mike.

## CHAPTER 31

"This doesn't make any sense," Dani says, pacing in front of the whiteboard to expend the nervous energy that's been building up inside her since she saw the picture of the girl under the ice. "The Snow Killer has been recreating that scene over and over here on the moors. Are we absolutely certain Robert North was in Spain when he says he was?"

Matt, who is still sitting in front of the computer, nods. "Henson's team checked and double-checked that he was there. Apparently, they even found photos on social media of him at a Christmas event in Benidorm with his parents."

"But if they carried out all the other tasks so

sloppily, why would they put so much work into checking North's whereabouts?"

"Because the old lady in the downstairs flat said he was dodgy. So the detectives made sure he was abroad and had nothing to do with Caroline Shields' disappearance."

Dani throws up her hands helplessly. It's no coincidence that Astrid Andersen's death in Norway has been painstakingly recreated here in Yorkshire almost twenty years later. "Our killer saw Astrid under the ice at the lake," she tells Matt. "He saw the scene exactly as it is in that photo. But if it isn't Robert North, I don't know who else to look at."

Matt's phone rings. He checks the screen before answering. "Sandra, what have you got?"

He listens and nods while Dani continues to pace back and forth along the width of the room.

When he finally ends the call, Matt says, "Sandra has spoken to the Norwegian police, Guv. Apparently, the oldest North boy didn't die in the accident after all. It was reported that he did because he didn't emerge from the lake with the rest of his family but the police found him the next day. He was sitting on the beach at the edge of the lake, right next to Astrid Andersen's body. He'd been there all night."

"It's him," Dani says. "What's his name? Where does he live?"

"This is the part you're not going to believe, Guv. His name is Michael North and he lives in the first floor flat at Northmoor House."

"What?" She grabs the case file and flips to the inquiry forms the constables filled out when they questioned the residents of the house. On the form for the first floor flat, the name written at the top of the page is *Mike Frost*.

"The sneaky bastard," Dani whispers.

"Guv?" Matt leans closer to look at the form.

She shows it to him. "He gave a false name. He probably knew they wouldn't check his ID. He's been under our noses the whole time. He sat next to Astrid Andersen's body all night and formed some sort of—" she closes her eyes, searching for the word Maya Cho used to describe an inappropriate sexual attachment. "Paraphilia. Then he sees Caroline dressed as Snow White, with a ribbon in her hair, and the paraphilia is triggered to a level he can't control. Come on, we need to go out there and pick him up."

They leave the room and as they make their

way along the corridor, she adds, "We're going to need a search warrant for the entirety of Northmoor House. And a SOCO team. I want every inch of that house searched. Get on the phone to HQ while I call Kate Lumley."

"Kate Lumley, Guv?"

"I have to tell her to get out of the house. She's just the type he goes for and look outside." She points at the snowstorm beyond the window. "This is exactly the type of weather that makes him strike."

## CHAPTER 32

*December 12th, 2002*

He saunters out of the hotel as slowly as he can, just to annoy his parents who are waiting at the car with Rob. He didn't want to come to Norway and look at stupid fjords. It's just boring. He wanted to stay at home and play *Grand Theft Auto: Vice City* on his PS2 but his dad insisted that they come and look at water and snow, like that's anything special. And since Mike is only twelve, he's not allowed to stay home alone, no matter how much he wants to.

"Come on, Mike," his dad says, "We're going to have our photo taken." He ushers Mike over to the red rental Volvo and makes him stand next to his brother. He's roped some local guy into taking their picture in front of the car.

Just to be awkward, Mike pulls up his scarf to cover his face.

Rob sees him and follows suit.

Mike rolls his eyes. His little brother is ridiculous.

"Say cheese," the man with Dad's camera says.

Mike doesn't say cheese. Instead, he whispers, "Piss off," his voice muffled by the scarf.

The guy hands the camera back to Dad and says, "Have a nice evening. Lake Femund is lovely at this time of year. But don't be out too long; the weather is closing in."

"Great," Mike mutters. "That's all we need, more stupid snow."

His mum gives him a light swat on the head. "Mike, don't be so ungrateful. We took you out of school early so you could see Norway. Would you rather be in class right now?"

He doesn't bother telling her that it's after six o' clock in the evening so he'd be home from school by now anyway. Besides, he thinks that maybe he *would* rather be at school. At least he'd be able to see Alice Clark.

He's been in the same classes as Alice for two

years but until this term started, he never really noticed her. In fact, he never would have paid her any attention because she's a girl but now his feeling towards girls are starting to change. He notices them much more now and thinks that maybe there's something about them that he really, really likes.

"Oh blast," Dad says. "That was the last of the film. Might as well leave the camera here." He starts walking to their hotel room.

Mike rolls his eyes again. If his Dad had a digital camera, instead of an old film one, this would never happen. Still, maybe he can use it to his advantage. "Hey, Dad, why don't we wait until tomorrow to go to the lake when you've got some more film? Not much point going there if you can't take pictures."

"There's plenty of point," his dad says. "We're not just here to take pictures, Mike. We're making memories."

Mike rolls his eyes yet again. He's afraid if he's forced to roll them much more, they'll fall out.

Dad drops the camera off in the hotel room and returns to the Volvo, swinging the keys in his hand. "Okay, let's go."

The weather closes in two hours later. Mike is sitting in the back of the car next to Rob while his dad looks at the road map. They're parked next to the lake. Dad got lost on the way here and now he's trying to bluff his way out of the fact that he doesn't know the way back to the hotel.

Mike is sure his dad hasn't actually got a clue and is only trying to make Mum feel better by pretending that he knows what the hell he's doing.

Bored with his dad's charade, he turns to look out of the window. The snow is falling so fast that he can't see anything out there.

"What are you looking at?" Rob asks.

"Nothing. Go back to sleep."

"I wasn't asleep."

"Well you should be you baby, it's past your bedtime."

"I'm not a baby, I'm eight." Rob leans forward. "Mum, tell Mike I'm not a baby."

Mum turns around in her seat. "You two stop arguing." She seems flustered and Mike realises that Dad's act isn't fooling her. She looks worried.

"Mike is calling me a baby," Rob whines.

Her expression grows angry. "Rob, be quiet.

Your father and I are trying to work out a way to get back to the hotel."

"Don't worry, it's all in hand," Dad says. "We just follow this road along the lake for awhile and then check the map again when we see a road sign or something."

Mum turns back to face forwards and gestures to the snow falling on the windscreen. "How are we going to see a road sign in this?"

"We'll be fine," he says. He starts the car and pulls onto the snow-covered road.

Mum grabs the edge of her seat as if she's riding a rollercoaster. "Slow down, Fred."

Dad doesn't slow down. There's a palpable atmosphere in the car that makes Mike sink into his seat. He's seen his Dad in this mood before and it isn't a good idea to cross him when he's like this. Instead of slowing down, Mike is sure his Dad has increased his speed.

"Fred, I said slow down."

Dad is silent. Illuminated by the dashboard lights, he seems hunched over the wheel, his face close to the windscreen as he tries to see the road ahead. In the beam from the headlights, snowflakes whirl and scatter like fireflies.

Suddenly, there's another light. This one

illuminates the interior of the car and Mike sees that his dad is indeed hunched over the wheel and his face is set into a grimace. The light is coming from the road ahead of them. A pair of headlights pointing straight at them.

Mum screams and Dad spins the steering wheel, the grimace now a look of panic. A terrible crunching sound fills the air and for a moment, Mike feels as if the world is spinning out of control. But it isn't the world that's spinning; it's the car.

Rob screams even louder than Mum and that's the last sound Mike hears before his head is slammed into the back of the passenger seat. A sudden blackness explodes into his vision and into his mind, blotting out everything else except for a feeling of cold so intense that it numbs his body.

When he regains consciousness, he's floating in dark water. Below him, in the murky depths, he can see car headlights. He wonders if Mum and Dad and Rob are down there, still buckled into their seats.

His lungs ache. He tries to swim up to the

surface but his arms are so cold he can't make them work properly. Or maybe it isn't just the cold; his jacket is torn and there's dark blood blossoming from his arms into the water around him.

The thought that he might be about to die doesn't really worry him. He's so numb—in his head as well as in his body—that his thoughts and emotions feel as if they're frozen. There's no sadness, no pain, and no fear.

He kicks his legs and gradually rises to the surface. There's ice here, thin sheets of it floating on the lake. Mike swims to shore, navigating a path around the ice until he's in water shallow enough that his feet touch the bottom. Then he walks out of the lake and stumbles along a snowy beach, unable to see much in the darkness.

He remembers seeing on a survival programme on telly that if you're cold, you have to keep moving. So he walks along the beach, trudging through the snow, and moves his shoulders back and forth until the feeling comes back into his arms.

As the night wears on, Mike keeps moving. He has no idea how far he's travelled and he's not sure if he's been walking for hours or minutes. He realises that if anyone is going to come and rescue him, they'll be at the site where the cars crashed into the lake so he turns around and begins to walk back that way.

But the snow obscures his vision and he's not sure he can find the crash site anymore. Not only that, he feels light-headed and weak. He needs to sit down or he might fall over. And he's sure that if he falls over, he'll never get back up.

Something in the water catches his eye. Something near the shore. He staggers over in that direction and his breath catches when he sees what lies under the ice.

He's never seen a dead body before but it isn't the fact that the woman under the ice is dead that shocks him; it's her beauty.

She's perfect. Locked under the ice and frozen in time. Mike falls to his knees, transfixed by the sight before him. Her eyes stare up at the snow-filled sky. He leans over her so that she's staring at him and he at her. He looks deep into blue eyes that will see no more. But it's her hair that enthralls him. Spreading around her head like a halo of golden fire, undulating with the movement of the water. And floating among that halo is a crimson ribbon as red and bright as fresh blood.

Mike sits with the sleeping angel all night. He drifts in and out of a dangerously deep slumber, sure that the woman under the ice is speaking to him in his dreams. He has no idea what she's saying but her voice is melodious and bewitching.

When morning arrives, the snow has stopped falling. A cold sun rises over the lake and Mike is sure that this is the last sunrise he will ever see. He's sitting in a pool of his own blood. It's been seeping out of him all night and now it stains the snow around him as bright crimson as the ribbon in the woman's hair.

He drifts into sleep again and the next time he awakes, someone is grabbing his arm. At first, he thinks he's died and it's the spirit of the woman under the ice lifting him up, taking him to Heaven with her.

But it isn't the woman at all. Two men are lifting him to his feet and on the road, he can see an ambulance, lights flashing and illuminating the snow.

He looks at the woman and tries to shake off the hands that are supporting him. He doesn't want to leave her.

As he's dragged towards the road and the ambulance, he tries to fight against the hands that hold him but he's too weak. Why can't they see that he wants to stay here?

He tries to keep his eyes fixed on the sleeping angel beneath the ice but he's bundled into the ambulance and the doors are slammed shut.

## CHAPTER 33

Mike stands in the middle of the road and looks from me to the Mini in the ditch. "What happened?"

"The wheel came off," I tell him. "Someone loosened it."

"Yeah, I saw it on the road back there. Are you okay?"

That simple question brings a new flood of tears. No, I'm not okay. There's a dead woman in our house and her parents—who were probably hoping and praying that their daughter was still alive—will have their hopes shattered when they find out her body was stuffed into a freezer in the attic above her own flat.

Mike sees I'm in distress and comes forward

to comfort me. I step back and wipe the tears from my face, holding up an arm to ward him off. "No, I'm fine." I refuse to break down until I can get word to the police about Caroline. She shouldn't be in that freezer any longer than she has to be.

Mike steps back and holds his arms up. "Sorry, I didn't mean—"

"It's fine," I say. "Can you give me a lift?"

"Of course, get in."

I climb into the Land Rover. Mike gets into the driver's seat and I notice that he's only wearing jeans and a black T-shirt that has a white logo of some heavy metal band on the front. He's hardly dressed for the weather.

Both of his arms are covered with a criss-cross of scars. At first I wonder if he's self-harmed at some point in his life but the jagged nature of the scars, as well as their chaotic arrangement on his arm, is nothing like the neat slashes I'd expect to see on the arms of a self-harmer.

"Aren't you cold?" I ask as he puts the Land Rover into gear and we continue down the road. He doesn't even have the heating turned on.

"I like the cold," he says.

*Why are you asking him about the cold when you*

*haven't asked him the obvious, burning question in your head?*

"Why are you driving Rob's car?"

"I use it sometimes. My car isn't so great in the snow."

"Really? But you have a Volvo. I would have thought that would handle the snow with no..." My voice trails away as I realise that Mike drives a red Volvo, the same as the one in the framed picture of the North family. It's a later model, of course, but it's exactly the same colour.

"I'm surprised he lets you use his car. You two don't really get on."

He shrugs. "We have our ups and downs like most brothers."

"Brothers?"

He nods. "Yeah, it's no secret. I just don't like to telegraph it. With him being so stupid, I mean. Best to let people assume we're not related, you know?"

I don't say anything. My mind is working through what I've just learned but I'm still confused. "I thought Rob's brother died in a car accident."

He grins. "No, everyone thought that at first but they found me the next day. I spent the night on the beach next to the lake, frozen half to death and sitting in a pool of my own blood."

"That must have been awful."

Mike shakes his head emphatically. "No, it was wonderful. The best night of my life."

I wonder if he's joking but there isn't a trace of sarcasm in his voice.

"I saw an angel that night," he says.

*You were probably hallucinating,* I think to myself.

"I don't mean I was seeing things," he says, as if he can read my mind. "There was an actual angel. We made a connection that goes beyond life and death. Do you know what I mean?"

I shake my head. I have no idea what he means and now he's beginning to scare me. All this talk of life, death, and angels makes me wish I'd stayed with the Mini and waited for someone else to come along.

"You might know soon," he says.

I have no idea what he means by that either. I shrink back in my seat, wondering if I should get out, maybe even jump out. Something isn't right here and it's more than the shock of finding out that Mike is Rob's brother.

Then I remember Mike's tracks in the snow on

the day I found him in the shed. They came from the back door.

He must have come from the attic that day. And the grey duct tape he got from the shed that day is the same tape I saw on the freezer earlier.

My blood runs cold. I had it wrong all along. The car that Ivy and I heard at night wasn't Rob at all; it was Mike using Rob's Land Rover. And the footsteps I heard in the attic were probably Mike's as well.

He looks over at me and smiles coldly. "I know you're not stupid, Kate. You're probably figuring some things out right now. You went to the press with that story about Rob because you thought the police would find evidence that he killed Caroline, right? You just started the ball rolling and expected the police investigation to do the rest."

I don't say anything. I'm trying to work out how fast I can get my seatbelt off and jump from the car. I have to make sure I don't injure myself in the process because after I land, I'm going to have to run.

After letting out a long sigh, he says, "I'm disappointed that you'd give Rob that much credit, to be honest. He doesn't have that much intelligence. They had to perform surgery on his brain after the accident and the result...well, you've seen the result. He's not exactly the sharpest tool in the box."

He looks over at me. "You're not saying much."

I need to bide my time, look for the right moment to jump from the Land Rover. A quick glance at the speedo tells me we're doing 35 miles per hour. I don't know how dangerous a jump at this speed will be. If I wait until Mike slows to go around a bend in the road, I might lessen the impact damage and that could mean the difference between life and death.

"Why did you do it, Mike?"

"I told you, I saw an angel when I was young and it was the most powerful experience of my life. A couple of years ago, I realised that I could recapture the rapture I felt that first time."

"By murdering women?"

"It isn't murder; it's a communion."

I don't even know what to say to someone who harbours that kind of madness. Up ahead, the road bends sharply to the right. He's going to have to slow down. To the left, in the direction I'll be trying to make my escape, the snow-shrouded moors seem to stretch into forever.

Dropping my hand to the seatbelt buckle, I prepare to press it.

The Land Rover reaches the bend and Mike slows down.

I release my seat belt and pull on my door handle.

The door doesn't open.

Mike shakes his head. "The doors are locked, Kate, there's no point trying to escape." His face darkens and he says, "I'm afraid there's no escape for either of us."

"What do you mean by that?"

After leaving the bend behind, he accelerates again. On our left, the moors flash by. On the right, I can see the cliffs and the sea.

"Rob didn't have much intelligence," Mike says, "but he did have a camera. I had no idea that the dirty little pervert was spying on Caroline. Even when he went to Spain to visit Mum and Dad, he kept the camera running. So when Caroline let me into her flat and I drowned her in her bath, the whole thing was recorded. Rob was furious when he returned home and saw what his stupid little camera had caught."

He laughs. "He really liked her. In fact, I think he was probably in love with her in his own sick way." His face darkens again and he becomes serious. "He didn't go to the police but he kept copies of the video on his computer and in the cloud. The police are going to find it now. And that's all thanks to you, Kate. You brought them to our door."

"Where are you taking me?" I ask.

He looks over at me and I see a profound sadness in his eyes that wasn't there before. "It isn't where I'm taking you, my angel, but where we're going together."

## CHAPTER 34

"Careful, Guv, there's a vehicle ahead," Matt says from the passenger seat. He's holding onto the handle above his door for dear life as they race along the road that leads to Northmoor House. There are two beat cars behind them, lights flashing and sirens wailing but even they're not matching the speed of the Land Rover Discovery.

Dani dare not slow down. She's sure Kate Lumley is in trouble. She can feel it in her bones. With her hands gripping the steering wheel so tightly that her knuckles are white, she's driven from Scarborough at breakneck speed, thankful that the bad weather has kept most motorists off the roads.

But there's always someone who is willing to

risk a drive out, despite weather warnings from the Met Office, and in front of her there's a green Land Rover on the opposite side of the road, heading towards her.

As soon as she sees it, Dani recognises the vehicle as belonging to Robert North. She'd tried to get a search warrant for the car but was only given one for his flat, as the courts decided the car had nothing to do with the voyeurism offence she was investigating. But she still remembers the number plate and unique pattern of dents and scrapes on the Land Rover and it's definitely the car driving towards her now.

"That's Robert North's car," she tells Matt.

He squints at it through the windscreen. "Yeah, it is."

Dani can see a male driver and female passenger in the approaching Land Rover but it's too far away to tell if it's Michael North and Kate Lumley. Her gut tells her that it must be. Who else would be in Robert North's Land Rover in this weather?

She applies the brakes and turns the wheel, letting the Discovery skid sideways so that it blocks both sides of the road.

Matt has gone rigid in his seat, his hand

gripping the handle above his head so tightly he might rip it off. "Guv, what are you doing?"

"I'm stopping a suspicious vehicle."

The beat cars behind them slow to a stop and turn off their sirens but leave their lights flashing.

Ahead, the green Land Rover skids to a stop. Dani can see the two occupants now. Michael North is in the driver's seat and a scared-looking Kate is sitting next to him.

Before Dani can get out of her car and advance towards the Land Rover on foot, North guns the engine and drives forward.

"He's going to ram us, Guv!" Matt shouts.

But before the vehicle reaches them, it veers off the road and kicks up snow and mud as it traverses the ditch and drives across a field that leads to the cliffs.

Dani slams the Discovery into gear and follows. "Hang on, Matt, it might get bumpy."

They bounce over the shallow ditch and Dani presses the accelerator shooting the car over the slippery field.

"What the hell is he doing, Guv?" Matt asks, looking as pale as a sheet.

Knowing what she knows about Michael North's trigger and desires, Dani is sure she can answer that question. The words she speaks next chill her. "He's going over the cliff and he's taking Kate Lumley with him."

Matt leans forward in his seat. "Step on it, Guv. We've got to stop him!"

O——⚿

I brace myself against the dashboard as we bump over the field, heading straight towards the cliffs. "Mike, what are you doing?"

Despite the fact that the police are chasing him, he seems composed and calm. "I'm completing a circle that started when I was a child. I was probably supposed to die in the lake with Astrid. In fact, I'm sure I *did* die that night in some way. She's been waiting for me, Kate. All that remains is for me to take the final step and I'll be with her forever."

In desperation, I pull on the door handle again but to no avail. "Mike, stop. You don't have to do this."

He nods. "Yeah, I do. I've been living on borrowed time since the accident and now it's time to pay my debt."

I look in the wing mirror and see DI Summer's

car behind us. I don't know what her plan is but she's probably not going to reach us before we go over the cliff edge.

I remember reading somewhere that if you're stuck inside a car, you can use the metal prongs in the headrest to break the window. I grab the headrest and pull on it with all my strength. It comes loose and ends up in my hands, the two metal prongs sticking out from beneath it.

I don't use it to break the window; I ram it into Mike's face.

He instinctively puts his arms up to defend himself and I take that opportunity to grab the steering wheel, pulling on it as hard as I can.

The Land Rover goes into a spin, churning up snow and mud.

Mike shouts something at me but I don't listen. I'm too busy jabbing the headrest prongs at him so that I can keep control of the steering wheel.

I know I don't have much time. Once he regains control, he'll turn us around again and head for the cliff.

The central locking is on a panel on his door. I reach across him and punch the button, hearing the locks disengage. He grabs me but I pull away from his grip and open my door. Cold air and snow rush inside the car and the wind blows the door closed again.

Mike reaches for the lock controls but before he can hit the button, I wrench my door open again and jump.

"Kate Lumley is out of the vehicle, Guv," Matt says. "She's on the ground."

"Hang on!" She turns in the direction of Kate and slams on the brakes. Unhooking her seatbelt, she gets out of the car.

"What about North, Guv?"

"Leave him for now. She may be injured." She runs over to Kate, who is lying prone, arms above her head, face hidden by the snow. She's holding a headrest in one hand, the prongs slick with blood.

"Kate!"

Kate stirs and rolls over onto her back before sitting up.

"Are you okay?" Dani visually checks Kate over. She's probably going to know about it in the morning when she's all bruised up but at the moment she looks fine, if a little shaken.

"He's going to kill himself," Kate says. "You

have to stop him."

Dani turns back to the Land Rover Defender. Both doors are open. Mike has left the vehicle and is walking towards the cliff edge. Matt is also on foot, running towards Mike and shouting, "Guv, he's going to jump."

Mike reaches the edge of the cliff and looks up at the snow-filled sky. He spreads his arms and throws his head back in what looks to Dani to be a religious gesture, as if Mike is commending his soul to God, the sky, the season, or whatever the hell he believes in.

Then he leans forwards and disappears over the cliff edge.

Matt tries to slow himself down and ends up sliding and falling onto his backside in the snow. He turns to Dani and shakes his head in despair.

Dani helps Kate to her feet and tells her to wait in the Discovery. Then she goes over to Matt and helps him to his feet before walking carefully to the cliff edge. Matt joins her and says solemnly, "There's no way he survived that fall, Guv."

"We'll get a team down there when the weather improves." Dani searches for any sign of North's body below but all she can see is the cold, rough sea beating against the rocks.

## CHAPTER 35

*One Week Later*

Dani sits at her desk watching DC Sandra Sharp take down the pictures from the boards on the wall and place them into a cardboard box. Some of those photographs have been up there for almost two years; scattered fragments of lives and deaths that have been examined and scrutinised endlessly in the search for the truth.

No one could have guessed that a car accident that took place almost twenty years ago in Norway would have such far-reaching repercussions and cause the deaths of five women.

"Weren't you supposed to go home an hour ago, Guv?" Matt is standing by her desk, a mug of steaming coffee in his hand, shirt sleeves rolled up.

Dani nods and rubs her eyes. Charlotte goes back to Uni tomorrow and Dani is supposed to take her to the Captain's Table again for a meal. She's been so busy with this case that she's barely seen her daughter the last few days.

"I'm going," she tells Matt as she gets out of her chair and grabs her coat.

He looks at the slowly-emptying board. "It's going to seem strange. Having a bare board, I mean."

"It won't be bare for long, you know that. There'll be a new case tomorrow. New pictures. New tragedy."

He nods slowly and takes a sip of his coffee. "At least the last one tied itself up neatly in the end."

Dani raises an eyebrow. "I don't think that what they found in the water beneath that cliff was very neat, Matt."

"Well, no, but at least justice was done."

"Was it?" She puts her coat on and gestures to the faces of the five women on the board. "Do you think their families would have wanted Michael North to kill himself or rot in jail?"

Matt shrugs. "I don't know. I suppose it all depends on their personal feelings about crime, punishment, and death."

"The important thing is that he can't do it again. It won't help the families of those five women but other lives have been saved. Lives we'll never know about. Women whose faces won't end up on that board."

She bids him goodnight and goes down the stairs to the ground floor before heading out to the car park. It's dark already, despite it being early evening, and there's a chill in the air. But at least there's no snow.

When she gets to the cottage, Barney and Jack run out to to greet her, barking and wagging their tails so hard that they look like they might be in danger of taking off like helicopters.

Charlotte stands at the door, arms folded, a smile on her face. Dani notices that her daughter is already made up and dressed for their evening out.

"Sorry I'm late, Charlie."

"Don't worry about it, Mum. I know you're busy."

"Yeah, but not so busy I can't spend time with my own daughter." She thinks of the five families who won't be able to spend time with their daughters ever again and hugs Charlotte tightly while the dogs whirl and prance around them.

## CHAPTER 36

I stand outside the main entrance of Northmoor House and watch the removal men bringing our furniture out of the house and loading it into their van. Greg is in the flat, coordinating things from there.

Tonight, we're staying in a hotel on the West Cliff and tomorrow, we're moving into a flat closer to town. We can't stay here after everything that happened, despite an email from Fred and Wanda North telling us we don't have to leave.

They must be devastated about what happened to their sons—Mike is dead and Rob has been charged with being an accessory after the fact to murder—so their email was generous, considering the circumstances, but I told them we were going.

I can't live in a flat where tragedy seems to linger in the air like floating cobwebs.

"Would you like a last cup of tea, dear?"

I turn to see Ivy standing in the hallway and nod. "That would be lovely, Ivy, but I told you, it won't be our last. I'll still come and visit you. We aren't going far."

She nods but seems dubious. Being let down by her daughters has made her cynical.

Following her into her flat, I say, "Looks like there are going to be some changes around here. New tenants. New management." The Norths sent a letter to Ivy informing her that they've hired a property management company to manage Northmoor House. "At least you might get repairs done faster."

"We'll see," she says, putting the kettle on. "I'm not getting my hopes up." She looks around the flat. "Where's Winston gone?"

"I think I saw him outside earlier."

"Oh dear. It's a bit cold out there for him."

"I'll find him," I offer.

"Here, take this." She opens a tin of tuna and hands it to me, along with a fork.

I go outside, following the removal men who are carrying our mattress. As they load it into the van, I go around the side of the house to the back garden and tap the tin with the fork.

Winston doesn't show so I call his name and tap the tin again.

There's a shout from the van. "It's that bloody cat again!" and I turn to see Winston leap out and run towards me, tail in the air like a ship's mast.

"Come on," I tell him, "Let's get you inside."

He follows me back to Ivy's flat where I find Greg sitting at the kitchen table, being served tea.

"Taking a break?" I ask him.

He nods and takes a biscuit from a plate Ivy holds out to him.

Later, after the removal men have gone and we've said goodbye to Ivy, Greg and I stand outside Northmoor House and take a look at the imposing structure in the evening gloom.

This was my dream flat, perfect in almost every way when we first moved in. Now, I'm happy to say goodbye.

"Are you ready to move on?" Greg asks.

I look at him and nod. "Yes, I'm ready to move on."

. . .

THE END

If you enjoyed The Red Ribbon Girls, you'll love Dark Peak by Adam J. Wright.

Download your copy HERE

Made in the USA
Las Vegas, NV
11 October 2023

78952600R00204